Henry Anderton

The Temperance

And other Poems of the late Henry Anderton

Henry Anderton

The Temperance
And other Poems of the late Henry Anderton

ISBN/EAN: 9783744765732

Printed in Europe, USA, Canada, Australia, Japan

Cover: Foto ©Andreas Hilbeck / pixelio.de

More available books at **www.hansebooks.com**

THE

TEMPERANCE

AND OTHER

POEMS

OF THE LATE

HENRY ANDERTON,

OF WALTON-LE-DALE, NEAR PRESTON,

WITH A SKETCH OF HIS LIFE,

BY HIS FRIEND AND FELLOW-LABOURER,

EDWARD GRUBB.

" Praise famous men, such as by their counsels, and knowledge of learning were meet for the people,—and were wise and eloquent in their instructions, and such as found out musical tunes, and recited verses in writing."—ECCLEASTICUS xliv. v. 1 and *seq.*

" A verse may find him who a sermon flies,
And turn delight into a sacrifice."
HERBERT.

PRESTON :
PRINTED BY W. AND J. DOBSON, FISHERGATE.
1863.

TO JOHN GUEST, ESQUIRE,

OF MOORGATE GRANGE, ROTHERHAM,

THE FAITHFUL PATRIOT AND STEADY FRIEND

OF

CIVIL AND RELIGIOUS FREEDOM,

WHOSE EXERTIONS TO CONSOLIDATE THE BASIS AND

EXTEND THE BLESSINGS OF THE TEMPERANCE REFORMATION

BY AN EFFICIENT

ADMINISTRATION AND ENLIGHTENED ADVOCACY,

AND SO TO IMPROVE THE

CONDITION AND ELEVATE THE CHARACTER OF THE PEOPLE,

ENCOURAGE THE PHILANTHROPIST TO ANTICIPATE

FROM FUTURE EXERTIONS MORE EXTENSIVE GOOD,

THIS

COLLECTION OF THE POEMS

OF

THE LATE HENRY ANDERTON,

ILLUSTRATIVE OF THE PRINCIPLES OF THE

FIRST TEMPERANCE REFORMERS, IS INSCRIBED

BY HIS FAITHFUL

AND OBEDIENT SERVANT,

THE EDITOR.

PREFACE.

I cannot allow this work to pass from my hands without a brief explanation of the circumstances which induced me to edit and incur the responsibilities of its publication.

A few weeks before his last illness, I saw Mr. Anderton; he was then, to all appearance, in his usual state of health; on the 17th of October, I heard by the merest chance that he was dead. At that time I was living in the quiet little village of Acton, near Nantwich, where intelligence of even more exciting events than the death of an individual seldom reached me till it had ceased to interest other people. I anxiously looked out for the temperance publications, hoping to find some honorable mention of Mr. Anderton's early labours. But I was surprised when I found that the conductors of the very publications which professed to be the organs of the movement, allowed such a circumstance as the sudden and unexpected removal from this life of one of the most gifted men who ever espoused their cause to pass without any particular notice. As one of his old friends I shared the desire of many that something should be done to preserve the memory of his excellent deeds and great talents.

During the whole time of my private visits to him, after his retirement from the platform, I never failed to urge him to prepare his
speeches and poems for publication, and though he never positively
refused to agree to my proposal, he always left the subject for future
consideration.   I knew that his speeches had been fully written out
before delivery in the Cockpit (the original Preston Temperance Hall),
and also that in their original composition he had attempted to con-
struct and finish the several parts according to the precepts of the great
masters of ancient eloquence.   He rested his claims to distinction
upon his speeches ; his poems cost him no labour, and were merely
employed to assist a certain portion of his hearers to retain the leading features of his arguments in a more familiar style.

Not having received any particulars of his illness or death in a
direct way, I wrote to his brother for information, and to ascertain
whether he, or any one else, had taken steps to bring his speeches
and poems before the Temperance friends, for whose instruction and
amusement they had been composed.   The matter appeared to me so
important, that I urged him to give the subject immediate attention.
There were some special reasons at the time why his friends should
have acted upon my suggestion, and these I did not fail to point out.
The peculiarity of his genius, vast as was the popular appreciation of
it, was a riddle that could not be solved without his speeches, and I
was anxious to see them in print, that we might be in a fit position to
determine "What constitutes an oration ?"   Knowing these to be of
great value as to their literary character, I offered my assistance and
co-operation to carry out to the fullest any wish the family or friends
might have in the matter.   To my letter his brother wrote as

follows :—" I fear much that Henry did not take care of any of his works. So far as I can judge it will be impossible to collect anything that would fill a volume."

Disappointed but not discouraged at this unexpected intelligence, I began to rely upon my own resources, and, after retracing the memory of early times, put myself into correspondence with such of our friends as I could think likely to possess copies of what he had written. Every one to whom I had written evinced their willingness to entrust all their little treasures to my keeping. The *Preston Chronicle* and the *Alliance Weekly News* rendered very valuable assistance in this search. Many of the original poems in this work have been obtained, through the publicity of the two papers named above from the United States, Canada, and Australia. The interval between the several arrivals has been great, indeed, one has come to hand whilst I have been writing this explanation. It now only remains for me to say to those friends who have shown their readiness to assist me by giving up the copies in their possession, that I have done my best to return the obligation by a well-printed and handsome volume. They will now clearly comprehend the difficulties which precluded the appearance of the work at an earlier date, and that the delay, which was unavoidable, has been an advantage. They will be able to see also that my offer to assist others forced upon me the alternative either to disappoint those who were anxious the poems should appear, or to take the responsibility of publishing them at my own risk.

I may remark, further, that many of the poems mentioned in the sketch of his life, are omitted in this collection. It is not necessary to give the reasons which guided my judgment in excluding them. The poems were all written before he became identified with the Temperance Reformation, and consequently, they can have no interest for those into whose hands this volume will mainly fall. Up to the period of my own college life, which began in the autumn of 1838, and ended in the spring of 1847, I had a perfect knowledge of all Mr. Anderton had written, and can, therefore, vouch for this being a perfect collection of his early Temperance poems. I am warranted in saying, on the authority of Mr. Miles Pennington, who has furnished original details since (which I would gladly insert did space permit), that he has not written anything on Temperance but what this volume contains. I now commit this work to the special protection and patronage of the friends of the late Henry Anderton; and as I have spared neither labour nor expense to honour his memory, so I confidently rely upon them, and all the true men and women of our glorious movement, to see well to it that I have not laboured in vain.

CONTENTS.

	PAGE.
Memoir of Anderton...	XIII
A Peep into the Tap-room and its Visitors	1
It's worth your while	3
To the Drunken Politician	5
To Drunkards...	7
The Joys of Drinking	8
The Purge	10
Up, and be doing, Lads...	11
Topers and Mopers	12
Oh! now for a Tug	13
A Farewell to Drunkenness	14
Never Touch, Lads!	16
The Robber, Liar, and Quack, as patronised by law...	17
Try, Lads, Try	20
Good News	22
The Lads of Bacup	23
A Temperance Address delivered at Fleetwood-on-Wyre	24
The doings of Jerry	27
What is a Sot?	28
Our Object is Grand!	30
Pins a-Piece	31
The Dead Weight	33
How Quiet the Publicans are	34
An Address to Christian Professors on behalf of Drunkards	35
A Simile, showing how John Bull's aching tooth may be cured	36
An Address to the Inhabitants of Todmorden	37

PAGE.

Lines on the 13th Anniversary of the Teetotal Birthday of Ambrose Brook   38

A Recitation for the 16th Anniversary of Ambrose Brook's Teetotalism   ...   39

An Address for the 20th Teetotal Anniversary of Ambrose Brook   ...   41

An Epistle to Ambrose Brook   42

To the same   43

Lines on the Death of a Friend   43

To Jemmy Fielding, a P.S.   44

We fear not the Number nor Might of our Foes   45

Advice to Drunkards   45

A Temperance Song   46

Fair Down.—A True Tale   48

Moderationers   50

Safety   52

Charge to the Onset   53

To Gadsby   53

To the Ladies   55

A Teetotaller's Song   56

The Temperance Hotel   57

Todmorden Lasses   58

Teetotal for ever shall Weather the Storm   58

A Hymn to be Sung at the Funeral of a Teetotaller   59

The Teetotallers' Advice to Drunkards   60

The Fellow who Cuddles his Tally   62

Lines written in an Album   63

Impromptu, on seeing some lines in an Album   64

Peep! A Panoramic View of Whig Legislation   64

To Mr. W. Harris   69

A new Song   72

Io Triumphe! or, Lord Duncan's Finale   74

Swig Away!   75

The Poor, God Bless 'Em!   76

A Water Drinker's Rhapsody   77

Railways and other Ways   78

Nature   79

CONTENTS. xi

PAGE.

Fleetwood-on-Wyre 80
Teetotalism in Harwood Lee 81
Song 83
Song 84
Teetotalism Triumphant 85
The Christian Poet 85
Lines on the Death of a Young Lady 86
To Elizabeth Mills, Rochdale 88
To a Friend, who trembled at the thought of dying 89
To a Young Lady from India 90
Lines on the Death of two Factory Children 91
The Sabbath 92
The "Nile" (steamer) 93
Stanzas to an old man on the Death of his only child 94
Stanzas on the Death of a Young Christian 96
To Little Hannah 96
To the same 97
To little Mary Langshaw 98
For Peter Langshaw, Jun. 98
Peter Langshaw 99
To Mary 99
To the same 100
To the same 101
To the same 102
To Fanny 103
To Mrs. Anderton 104
To Miss A. D. 105
To Margaret 106
Lines addressed to the Widow and Daughter of the late Richard Stephenson 107
To —— and his Sisters on the Sudden Death of their Parents 109
On the Death of a Young Friend 110
Ruth Johnson Bland, æt. 21 111
To Mr. Robert Snape 112
Love Song 114

PAGE.

Thirst, and its true Antidote 115

Song 115

A Blessing 116

A Blessing 117

Hymns sung on the occasion of laying the Foundation Stone of the
Temperance Hall, Bolton, May 24th, 1839 117

Hymn for Good Friday 119

A Hymn.—"Rejoice in the Lord alway."... 121

A Hymn 121

Evening Hymn 122

The River of Death 123

The Triumphs of Sobriety ... ... ' 124

An Appeal to the true Friends of Zion 125

What is a Drunkard 127

The Drunkard's Wife 128

The Dying Drunkard 129

To the Drunkard... 130

Appeal to Christians 131

Christian Expedience 132

Christian Efforts to re-claim the Intemperate... 134

The Drunkard Raised 135

Christ Died for Drunkards... 135

Appeal to Drunkards 136

MEMOIR OF HENRY ANDERTON.

THOUGH the poems of Henry Anderton have made his name known to the members of Temperance Societies all over the country, and he himself was personally known in most parts of Lancashire as one who took a prominent part in spreading abroad the knowledge of temperance principles, little or nothing is known of his private life beyond the circles of his friends. As one of the first of those men whose names are associated with the propagation, if not the actual discovery, of a great principle, his labours possess, in some measure, an historic interest. It is felt, at the present time, by all who remember him, that of all those who are regarded as the representative men of the temperance reformation in its first stages of development, not one ever obtained popularity by a life more pure, or a genius so commanding, or will retain it better as the cause advances, than Henry Anderton. The time he devoted to the advocacy of the cause, and the extent of ground travelled by him in diffusing a knowledge of the principles of the Preston men, was considerably less than some of his companions; but during the short period he devoted himself to the work he had uudertaken, he had no equal in the quality and amount of service rendered. This was the unanimous verdict at a time when the eventful scenes of the temperance reformation were such as tried the patience, roused the courage, and called forth the abilities of all who took part in the work. He was no skulker in these trying times, but took his place in the front ranks with its early champions, and intrepidly defended them and their cause with an eloquence and boldness that soon won over the multitude, and silenced the insolence of more cunning foes. Whatever opinions men held respecting the cause they advocated, they were compelled to admit that its success was mainly owing to the high moral character and extraordinary abilities of its advocates. Henry Anderton retains to this day the first place in the memory of those who have survived him, as the most eminent of all our early men. It is with a desire to gratify those who admired him when living, and to discharge the obligations which a sense of duty renders absolute, that I venture to supply a few particulars respecting him not generally known.

Henry Anderton was the second son of James and Ellen Anderton, of Walton-le-dale, near Preston, Lancashire. He was one of a family of eight children, all of whom exhibited, in early life, many marks of genius like their brother Henry. The principal aim of Mr. and Mrs. Anderton was to secure for their children a good education. With this view they sent Henry, when very young, to the National School, in Walton-le-dale, at that time conducted by a very able teacher, Mr. Robinson, the same gentleman who, at a later period, kept a noted school in Preston. For some time after young Anderton had been at school, Mr. Robinson was at a loss what to do with him. He was a very shrewd man, as well as a clever teacher, and he had never failed before in finding out the methods of his young pupils, but he was so baffled by Henry's strange manners as to give up the attempt in despair. On one occasion he went to his mother, and said, "I don't know what to make of your Henry; when I ask him a question he turns his back upon me, and yet I would give anything if the other lads had heads like your boy." When Mr. Robinson left Walton, Henry was removed to a school at Salwick, and from that place he was transferred to the care of Mr. Sedgwick, of Preston.

Mrs. Anderton's maiden name was Turner; she was born at Leyland, near Preston. I paid her a visit in March, 1859, when she had completed the seventy-seventh year of her age, and she appeared then, when talking about her boy, as vivacious as a young woman of thirty. She felt very grateful for the sketch and portrait of her son, in the *Spectator*, and requested me to convey her thanks to the parties connected with that work, for the kindly notice of her dear lad. I told her it might have been more worthy of him if his own friends had taken the trouble to furnish fuller information respecting his early life. She said, "I am not sure that they could have given much additional information ; what is stated is true, and given in such a way that I fancied my poor boy living again before my eyes." Her tears stopped her utterance ; when she recovered herself, she went on to say, "He was the queerest lad in the world, always in books, and, if we asked him what he was doing, we never could get an answer, he seemed so absent. He used to sketch pictures of dogs and other animals, to show the tricks and habits of the brutes. We wondered many a time where the lad got such notions; the pictures were so droll, our sides were nearly split with laughing at them. He was a very queer lad and his ways were odd, but, like Mrs. Ashcroft, what he did would bide looking into. You know how happy he was in *naming* his acquaintances, he had the same talent when a lad, for he found a name for every one. Not only what *he did*, but what he said, would bide looking in. You know what a commotion there was about Miss ——. Henry would never have a particle of charity for any man that was false to a woman. In that case he took her part as though she had been his own sister, and he said to —— 'If you do not marry that lass, you shall never see my face again.' "

Henry's maternal grandmother was a poetess, and, in some other respects, he inherited her characteristics. Mrs. Turner was, however, a Roman Catholic, while Henry imbibed, from his father, a dislike of Roman Catholicism. When little more than three years old, he was lost. Inquiries were made of the children playing about, but neither they nor any of the neighbours had seen him that day. Mrs. Anderton became greatly alarmed, and concluded that he must have fallen into the Ribble. Acting upon that conviction, she had the river dragged, but not finding him there, she ran up Church-brow, crying wildly like one deranged. The neighbours had, in the meantime, ascertained, from his sisters, where he was, and ran after her to tell her that Henry was found, and safe from harm. She flew back, and found him in her own bed, fast asleep, his finger resting on one of the pictures of the family Bible. She was so delighted at finding him, that she promised him a new beaver hat, that being an article he had often asked for. The hat was soon bought, but, when he once got possession, nothing they could do or say could prevail upon him to give it up. He lived in it in the day, slept in it at night, and wore it out in a week'. These little matters may appear trivial to some, but those who knew Anderton, as a man, will readily discover in such incidents the indications of some of those peculiarities which distinguished him through life. He was, from his childhood, fond of books. Indeed, so strong was his desire for knowledge, that he could not be prevailed upon to join in the little amusements and rougher sports of his companions. He would steal from them and wander alone in the fields, or play by himself on the banks of the Ribble. This musing turn of mind and aversion to play were ascribed to a feeble state of body, which unfitted him for enjoying such play as required physical strength, but this was soon found to be an erroneous conjecture. When about twelve years old, a party of young people called at his mother's house, and related to the family some very exciting particulars respecting the revival services in Vaux-hall Chapel, Preston. Sketches of the characters of some of the individuals who had been converted by the preaching of Mr. Moses Holden, the astronomer, were given by some of the young women. The narrative of these conversions, heightened as it was by the intense enthusiasm of the speakers, so roused the curiosity of the family, that they all felt a desire to see the same things them-selves. Mrs. Anderton gave her consent for James and some of the girls to go, but Henry, on account of his tender age, was to remain at home. No one had been so much interested in the strange history of the men whose lives had been described in such graphic colours ; he had been silent all the time, fixing his eyes stedfastly upon his mother's countenance ; he besought her to allow him to make one of the party. The young people, touched by his earnest manner, the music of his voice, and the unusual eloquence of his action, added their joint entreaty to his own request. His mother told him he was not able to walk so far, and that he was too young to understand such a man as Moses Holden. The young person whose narrative of the converted had awakened his desire, said that she "had known *many* who were no older than Henry, and not half as wise, who had been converted, and that no one could be converted without knowing it." She continued, "Who can tell, if he went with us, but that *he* might be converted this very night ? I think by his look, and those other signs he made, that he is partly converted now !" Henry flew to the damsel, and kissed her for the speech she had made in his favour, and then fixing his gaze

upon his mother's face, he pleaded his own cause in the following extempore
verses :—

> 'And after having ta'en such pains,
>   Must I on pins keep sitting?
> And will she keep my poor crack'd brains
>   By sad conjecture splitting?
>
> And can a mother use me so,—
>   Can she her feelings smother?
> Will she let James to Preston go,
>   And keep at home the other?
>
> No, mother, no! it's not thy mind;
>   Thou canst not deal thus badly;
> And thy pure heart is much too kind
>   To use a brute beast sadly:
>
> Much less treat ill thy weakly son;
>   'Twould be above digestion;
> Thouldst rather say, "Put thy clothes on,
>   And have a walk to Preston!"
>
> This is thy heart, I wot;
>   O may these lines impress thee!
> And whether I'm to go or not,
>   May God Almighty bless thee!

I give the piece as it came from his lips, because it was his first attempt at
rhyme, and also because the poet himself was more delighted with it than with anything he composed in his riper years. He gained his point, and from that
moment he grew more attractive to his relatives and friends. His young companions now looked upon him as a youth of very superior talents and ever after
hailed him by the title of poet.

I have now before me a collection of his poems, some written a few days
after the above address to his mother, and all appear to have been composed
within three years from that time. The whole are interesting in this respect;
they indicate the natural progress of his mind, and shew the methods he took
to nourish his genius and improve himself in the art of composition. The young
person who pleaded his cause so urgently, appears to have had a tolerably good
idea of his susceptible nature. I cannot gather from the manuscript volume
before me whether he was really converted that evening or not, but it was
abundantly evident that the sermon, and the excitement that followed, had a
most powerful effect upon his mind. The week following he composed a poem,
addressed to the Vauxhall preachers, giving them a poet's encouragement "to
preach without money the life-giving word." One of them was taken ill, and he
sent him a copy of verses to console him in his affliction. Several of his poems
in the collection, written about the same time, are addressed to various members
of the congregation, one on his own birth-day, and several birth-day pieces to
the members of his own family. "Walton-le-dale," a rural sketch, is his first

attempt at description of natural scenery. A poem to a young man entering on the work of the ministry in the Primitive connection, "Mystic Babylon," a poetical sketch of the Reformation, shows that he had acquired, by reading, a good knowledge of the facts relating to that great historical event. The characters of the leading men are well drawn, the style bold, the versification smooth and musical; but the poem, as a whole, is too one-sided. The chapel closed, and the people who assembled there separated; the reason is not stated, but it caused the worshippers great sorrow to be deprived of their place of meeting. Anderton, before leaving them, composed a song to "cheer them in the wilderness."

I am unable to furnish particulars of this religious movement, neither do I know exactly when the services finally closed; but I know this,—the impressions made upon Anderton in that society continued to influence him, more or less, to the end of his life. The little church broken up, a state of repose followed,—the memory of previous excitement faded like the recollection of a dream. The charm of association was lost by the dispersion of those whose presence awakened his enthusiasm,—to supply its loss and preserve the flickering pictures of his fancy, he betook himself to the fields and groves. He found in the solitude of nature that stimulus to his imagination which before came from the living crowd. Withdrawn from society, and the senses open to the voice of nature, his mind was wholly absorbed in the study of natural objects. Now, the flowers appeared to have new beauties to please the eye; the ingenuity of birds to rival the workmanship of man; and the murmuring stream and the howling winds composed or roused his emotions by an unknown spell. He discovers within an increase of strength, and now, for the first time, tried the fancy in a new sphere of picture-making. His first experiment as a satirist was in a poem entitled "The Lodge," a tale in two parts. This was soon followed by others of the same character; one, "Look before you Leap, or Tom and Cicely," and another, a very clever burlesque, called "Tabby's Lilies." By some means the drift of the tales got into circulation, and, as the people were known, it caused some annoyance; provoking the parties to threaten the poet with correction, which, for a time, made the young rhymer look out for his own safety. He had a good circle of friends about his own age, who greatly admired his talents. As many of these were young women, they gradually drew his attention from personal satire to themes more pleasing. He kept up an extensive correspondence with these young people, no doubt as much for his own improvement as their gratification. He now began song-writing. The songs addressed to the young women display many delicate touches of fancy, and show that he had acquired great power of expression. In time, the number of his acquaintance grew less as they advanced in years and went forth to engage in the duties of active life. His father died, and Henry was the one on whose efforts the family had now, in some measure, to depend.

It may be mentioned here that, either from his reading or the influence of others, he had, by this time, imbibed strong political opinions. So greatly did these operate, that for a long time questions of a political character were the only topics in which he took any interest. The working population of Lancashire have always shown a partiality for politics; and the people of Preston were then considered more inclined in that direction than those of any other part of the country. Be that as it may, the social tendencies there were very strong, and the political privileges of the place helped to keep alive and strengthen the sympathies of the people. They were ever ready, in times of danger, to defend the common cause; none more prompt in the promotion, or more rapid in the development of political associations, when political intriguers assailed the principles of the constitution. Before the formation of temperance societies, questions of a civil nature were paramount to all others, and the only questions in which the people took any particular interest. Much of the intemperance of that period arose out of such political combinations as then existed. Mechanics' Institutions were then in their infancy, and, as they excluded politics, the people regarded them with suspicion. As books and newspapers were above the means of the poor, they flocked to the tavern to hear the news. Drinking, with them, was, in the first instance, made a condition merely to the gratification of a nobler desire. The success of the publican depended more upon his company as a political consideration, and on his having a good reader for his paper, than on the colour or strength of his liquor.

Before the passing of the Reform Act, a powerful political association existed in Preston. The town was divided into districts, each of which comprehended a section of the whole union. The meetings were held at some public-house in the district. The most important gatherings took place on the Sunday evenings. Here the newspapers were read, the members attending with as great exactness as though it had been a place of worship. At first it was not the general custom to drink during the delivery of an address, or when the most important part of the papers was being read; but every one was expected to drink or pay before leaving, for the good of the house. But that custom soon gave way; and thus it happened that meetings intended for the information of the people had a most demoralizing effect. The use of intoxicating liquors defeated every attempt to improve the worst, and many of the best men thereby became intemperate. The fearful increase of a vice which, from so small a beginning, at first made its victims from the least cautious, had now made its attacks upon the stout in purpose. Drunkenness was no longer a solitary vice confined to special age, condition, or habit, but a general infatuation. It rose like a sudden flood, and carried all before it, with the resistless force of a torrent. All moral power was gone; and though mirth and misery mocked the victims of delusion, to resist or fly from the place of sin was impossible. The next change was to substitute religious for political topics. Infidel publications took the place of the old Radical prints, and by this contrivance the debauched attempted to gain a respite to their misery. At this dreadful stage of drunkenness and impiety, Anderton exerted all his noble faculties to check the ruling madness, and though he did not fully accomplish his desire, he never appeared in any conflict with so much advantage.

His first attempt was to get the members to prohibit the use of drink during the hours of business, and instead of the compulsory rule to drink for the benefit of the house, for each to pay a small sum for the use of the room. These suggestions, to some extent, were acted upon; and, in order to give a better tone, he advised a change in the publications. Having gained these points, and in the

hope of rooting out the infidelity that had come among them, he proposed that
sermons should be preached in the public-houses every Sunday evening, instead
of the usual reading and discussion. This also was agreed to as an experiment;
and to show them how to do it, he delivered a course of sermons on political
topics. His abilities carried him through, but the distaste of his audience for
anything having the semblance of religion brought the sermons to a close.
Anderton was resolved to abide by his original purpose, and, if defeated, take
the consequences. A party was soon formed against the poet and his sermons,
—a special meeting of the members was called,—a resolution submitted to the
effect that the publications which had been excluded be again introduced,
that no more sermons be delivered, and that the old mode of paying for the
room, by the drink, bo the general rule. This resolution was carried in the
division to which Anderton belonged. He made a vigorous address before the
resolution was put to the meeting, pointing out, in a wonderful strain of
eloquence, the bad consequences that had happened by following the rule recom-
mended for their adoption. But all was of no use; the opposition had taken
such precautions that no eloquence could prevail against it. Anderton again
rose, and in a few words requested his name to be taken off the books, and
called upon all who shared his views to leave the company. Many in that
meeting admired and loved him, and they left with him.

  In the meantime he devised another plan of association upon a new principle.
He suggested that all who had left with him should keep together, but instead of
meeting at a public-house they should assemble in small parties at the homes of
the members. It was further proposed that each individual should begin a
regular course of reading, and thus come prepared to enter upon the examina-
tion of the book when read at the private meeting. Tea was to bo provided, and
the expenses defrayed by the party visiting. In the society they had left, men
only were admitted; in this new family association, wives accompanied their
husbands, and young men brought their sweethearts. Though no means were
taken to add to the original number, his new scheme became well known, and
so popular that there was hardly a district in the town that had not its small
party. From this new arrangement sprang many direct advantages, and much
evil was prevented. It drew from the haunts of vice many who, but for his
example, would have been ruined. Young people of both sexes met at public-
houses; to prevent that, he devised his plan for the admission of young women
to these little friendly meetings. The change for the better was soon visible in
the improved moral character of that portion of the working population. Its
good effects were not confined to the members of these literary gatherings, but
extended to the workshops of the people. In short, in what place soever any of
these young people were called to act, they attempted the improvement of their
companions. Many who before had frequented the ale-house for the sake of
news, clubbed their pence together for a daily paper. In some shops books were
added as a shop library; the workmen appointed a reader, and, as a compensa-
tion, either worked for him during reading time, or paid him an equivalent in
money. During this period he wrote a good deal for the Radical papers; I
subjoin the titles of some of his political songs, which will convey a good idea of
his politics:—"To Free-born Englishmen;" "To the Spy;" "A Radical

Hymn ;" "A Republican Song," (tune,—"King of the Cannibal Islands'"); "The Jolly Tars ;" "Political Squibs ;" "The Monarch of Mind ;" "Kings are but Men ;" "The Poor, God Bless 'em !"

Anderton, towards the close of the labours spoken of in the former part of this sketch (the formation of an association on a new plan), paid a visit to some friends at Eccles, near Manchester, and during his stay with them he became a member of the Temperance Society in that place. A new and more beautiful prospect at once opened to his view. He saw more clearly than ever the means by which the poor might avoid a thousand snares.

His first appearance as an advocate was the commencement of a style of speaking which, for many years after, made the Preston Cockpit a school for eloquence. His first address was a victory to the cause itself; it secured for the infant institution a power and popularity that dazzled the imagination. He was then in the full bloom of early manhood, and to an original greatness of mind he brought with him into our ranks the lessons of experience only known to himself. From the first day to the last appearance he made upon our platform, he was the supreme attraction at all meetings of the temperance reformers. No man ever loved the people with a truer passion, or served them better. He surveyed everything with the eye of a philosopher, and poured forth his thoughts like a poet ; hence nature, as sketched by him, appeared like a new creation. It was not merely his knowledge of the natural world, the beauties that adorn it, the remote or striking analogies that mark the oneness of a Divine plan, that made him sole master of the judgment. He had made man his study. No metaphysician could better map out or classify the phenomena of the human mind ; it was that which gave his language the power and voice of nature. His speeches were prose poems, and his poems are little speeches, constructed with great regard to logical exactness. He travelled most parts of Lancashire, and visited a few towns in Yorkshire and Cheshire, mostly on foot, except where the distance was too great. He frequently walked from Preston to Manchester, and spoke the same evening ; the same to Todmorden.

As we are now drawing to a period when that change in temperance efforts began, which has gradually effaced the old principles, and created a new class of orators, we shall give two of his letters complete, and an extract from another, to show the beginning of troubles :—

"Walton-le-dale.

"Thou Canny Son of *Auld Reekie*,—Have the kindness to inform me whether or not you will have any public extra temperance meetings on Christmas-day ; because, if you have, I can return negative replies to several pressing invitations from elsewhere. I have a warmer side for Colne than I have for any other place, and, on that account, it has the preference of my humble services. Write by next post. Our cause is universally gaining ground. God is on our side. Hallelujah !

" 'Join our glad chorus of triumph and glee,
            Our cause is victorious—the drunkard is free.'

"My love to all good men and true, and tell them that, though 'my wheel is almost broken at the cistern,' I could wish to come and give another blow at the hell-planted Upas-tree of drunkenness ! Hurrah ! What thou doest, do quickly, and, by so doing, thou wilt confer an obligation on, my dear Scotchman, thine always and truly, "H. ANDERTON.

"N.B.—Direct for Henry Anderton, saddler."

"Preston, ———.

"Dear Douglas,—I cry shame to myself for my negligence in not sooner replying to the kind invitation of so dear a friend; for Scotchman though he be, and you know my national prejudices, yet, if I have rightly analysed my own feelings, there are few men whom I do love, and have cause to love, more than the honest, unsophisticated 'Sawney' whom I now address. Your letter brought to my recollection the days we have spent together; 'the rise and progress' of that society of which I was an humble instrument of raising into prosperity, and which you, through 'evil and good report,' have striven to keep together; and I should have been most happy to have been amongst you once more for the sake of 'auld lang syne,' but as I am expecting to be called away to a new situation, I must decline an invitation, which, on many accounts, it would have given me such unmingled pleasure to accept. I cannot name my Colne friends individually, they are so many; but to all give my heartiest well-wishes. I may come to see you, as Burns says, 'when simmer days are fine;' but, whether or not, that 'God may be thy guide through life, and thy portion for ever,' is the prayer of yours, stedfastly and teetotally, "HENRY ANDERTON.

"P.S.—I am not a saddler; I have given up business altogether. Tee-totalism drove my trade away. I shall be * * * and better off, I hope, in a short time. Good-bye!"

The improvements effected in our social habits by the formation of temperance societies are too obvious to require recital in this place. But the circumstances which led to their formation will never fail to interest those who take a pleasure in witnessing the efforts of the people for their own improvement. The curiosity of the benevolent should not rest satisfied at this point; they should extend their observations beyond the narrow limits of institutional arrangements, if they wish to acquire a knowledge of the men who carried out the principles of which such institutions are but the name. When the obstacles which beset the early advocates are fully comprehended, the diffusion of their opinions, and the partial triumph of their cause, in the face of such passionate and interested opposition, will appear more extraordinary than they had any notion of before. As the same circumstances do not exist at present, and, perhaps, never can exist again in this country, so there can be no comparison made between the Preston men of the early date and the advocates'of the present day. No doubt, the passions of mankind are the same now as then, but the opposition to which they urge men changes its character with the altered state of society. The simple and illiterate are still liable to be the dupes of the base and cunning, but the breadth of soil illuminated by the rays of truth has dispelled the bigotry and blindness of numbers. There is something awfully trying to a man's courage in the mere solitude of opinion. The Preston men experienced this oppressive solitude, for they stood alone, the solitary champions of a despised theory; their own friends, as well as their fellow citizens, were in arms against them, and they knew of none to whom they could appeal for sympathy or support. And yet these hard times to them were made the means of success. The postscript in the letter to

Mr. Douglas makes known, in a very few words, one form of opposition, to some men very convincing, but it failed in its effect upon Henry Anderton. When knaves and fools cannot bend honest men to their purpose, they try to starve them into submission. The publicans tried this "bread and cheese" logic with the poet of our movement, but it failed to silence him. He preferred to endure all the privations the withdrawal of their support might entail upon him, rather than submit to dishonourable conditions. At the time when the reformation commenced in Preston, the publicans were a more influential body of men than they are at present. The extension of the railway system had not infringed their monopoly of the road, and, as proprietors of the coaches, the business of a saddler was, to a large extent, derived from them. The interval between his first and last letter to Mr. Douglas was not a very long one, but mark the sudden change. In the first place, he is a saddler, in the last—nothing, a man without occupation. "Teetotalism drove my trade away," is the mournful carol he warbles in the ears of his friend. His genius and his virtue were his ruin. To understand the full extent of the suffering he endured at that time, through loss of business, is impossible. It did not involve mere privations of comforts to himself alone; his widowed mother and her fatherless daughters were involved in the same catastrophe. The greatness of his character appeared to eminent advantage at this critical period. Long before this happened, he had shown how he could think and act in very trying and unlooked for circumstances, but the time now arrived when he had to show his brother advocates how he had learned to suffer. His example proved a lesson to them, and it may yet be of use to those who may come after him. There is no growl of complaint in the announcement of his ruin,—he hopes, even against hope, that "soon he will be better off." I regret to have to state, that what he thought likely did not come to his relief so soon as he expected. Yet he never abandoned himself to despair; neither did his long-deferred hope of better times relax the efforts of his will; he did not quail before the insolence of his oppressors, nor forsake the cause of truth, because it did not enrich himself. He made no parade of his poverty, but submitted to his fate in silence. Whatever may have been his wants he asked for nothing, and he got as much. During his state of isolation from business, he was invited by some friends to pay them a visit. He could not be prevailed upon to go by the coach; he said, "I can foot it easily enough." By the time he had finished his journey, his shoes had given way. Such a disaster as that would ruin an advocate of the present day, at least, it would get him no shoes. But, in Anderton's time, an advocate meant something more than boots, brushes, and bear's grease, and as the loss of a shoe never detracts from the character of a good horse, so a good advocate, in his time, lost nothing of his inches from want of leather. In the state described, he made his appearance in the shop of Mr. Gandy, whose benevolent eye soon discovered the poet's damaged shoes, and, being skilled in the craft, soon supplied him with a better fit. I am sure that the performance of that noiseless action, done in a way that left no sting behind it, has returned to the doer of it a thousand blessings.

Among those who distinguished themselves by their extraordinary zeal in the cause of temperance in these early times, it would be an act of ingratitude not to mention the family of Mr. Phillips, of Warrington. They were just the people wanted at a time when the cause had to win its way to popular acceptance by the personal merits of its friends. They were a pious family, and in the propagation and vindication of their religion had been accustomed to persecution. In their day, camp meetings had been as unpopular as temperance meetings, so that they were not scared by the cry of unpopularity. The young men were sober, talented, and brave, fond of music, and, besides being well skilled in the use of instruments, could compose well. The young women, to great personal beauty added many accomplishments, and, like their brothers, were passionately fond of music, and were exquisite singers. I have noticed before the partiality of the working population of Lancashire for political enquiries, and it is well known that their partiality for music and eloquence was not less general at that time. The popular taste in both instances was the result of cultivation, and originated from a peculiar combination of circumstances, that had no existence elsewhere. This was of some advantage to the men who espoused unpopular views, for who ever excelled in either of these refined accomplishments was sure, in the end, to attach to himself friends and admirers. Perhaps the greatest mark of respect ever paid to Anderton was shown by this family. Next to the Cockpit, the Old Friar's Green Chapel, in Warrington, deserves to be associated with his name as one of the places where he displayed that mighty eloquence that touched all hearts and filled every eye. We have seen that he was invited to Warrington in the usual way, and in what state he arrived there—tired and shoes worn out. He had no idea that anything unusual was to occur during this visit, and having left Mr. Gandy he went direct to the house of Mr. Phillips. They were delighted to see him, and omitted no graceful attention to convince him that his presence added to their happiness. But they gave no sign that any particular token of esteem was the end proposed by the invitation. As the time for the meeting approached the young men went to make the necessary preparations, and Anderton had to go with their sisters. When they reached the chapel, Anderton was astonished at the sight of a full band of musicians, who began to play his own "Pins a Piece," which had been set to music for the occasion. I have heard him say that he was never so affected in his life before, and till that evening never fully comprehended that humour and pathos belonged to musical sounds. Many of the best of his poems were addressed to the family I have named. There are other old friends in Warrington who are entitled to be named as real friends to Anderton ; and though I have named the family of Mr. Phillips, on account of the special interest they took in everything relating to his happiness, I must associate with them the names of Mr. John Gandy and Mr. William Mee. The ladies had, unknown to others, collected among themselves a private token of their regard, and it was to their timely benevolence at this time that the poet was enabled to get through the difficulties that threatened for a time to overwhelm him.

Anderton, when writing to his familiar friends, usually expressed the substance of his letter in a copy of verses at the end. He adopted the same plan in his speeches, and hence the poems may be considered as the syllabus, in measured syllables, of his prose orations. The following letter will illustrate his method in this respect, and it is valuable also as making known the result of the impressions created in his mind by the religious services spoken of in the early part of this sketch. It was written to Mrs. Langshaw, eldest daughter of Mr. Phillips. He had been disabled from speaking for some time, and to her inquiry as to the cause, he returned this answer :—

Dear Mrs. Langshaw,

You will have thought me very neglectful and ungrateful in not answering your letter in better time, but I put it off till I could, *free of expense*, send the several members of your family some of my attempts at rhyme, as a keep sake from an unworthy but sincere friend, whom very likely they will never see again on this side *eternity.* I am still " a real staunch teetotaller, one of the present time," *though no longer a public advocate.* So are all our family from the least to the greatest. The reason why I do not speak and travel, as usual, are—first, my attendance is required at home ; and, secondly, because my voice was so injured with too much speaking, that I was obliged, for my life's sake, to take some rest. With the exception of preaching occasionally for the Methodists, with whom I am connected, I have been silent for some time, and so great is the benefit I have derived from this rest that last week I delivered a lecture on the " Spread of Knowledge," in Preston, which occupied one hour and a half, with perfect ease. . . . . . Will you give mine and my friends' love to all your " kith and kin."

> First give my love (no word is sweeter)
> To Mr. Stuff-a-Collar, Peter ;
> Next to your father and your mother,
> And then to Joshua, their brother ;
> Then show my heart, with right good will,
> To that prime grinner, brother Bill ;
> And next—the compliment to vary—
> Hand my regards to sister Mary.
> If Peter's back from Paddy's land,
> Give him, instead of mine, your hand ;
> And though of him I little know,
> Remember me to brother Joe.
> And when I come your face I'll smack,
> If you pass over Trombone Jack ;
> And she'd be angry if I miss'd;her,
> So don't pass o'er your youngest sister.
> While you this business are upon,
> I charge you not to pass by one,
> Not one kind friend that I have seen
> At Bridge-street or in Friar's Green ;
> And it would fill my heart with pain,
> To pass by thee, kind-hearted Jane ;
> You're all my friends, young, old, great, small,
> And I am yours—*God bless you all !*

The high postage charge upon letters was an obstacle in the way of frequent correspondence to one like Anderton, whose means were so limited. The hardship was great to him and the other advocates, for they not unfrequently spent the wages of a day's work in postage alone. So keenly was this felt, that it became necessary, in self-defence, either to refuse replies or wait the opportunity of some one going in the direction from whence the letters came. Everybody, more or less, felt the inconvenience of the old postage system, and, to relieve each other, they gave intimations of their intended journey, and asked if they had "any message to send." In this way Anderton sent most of his poems to private friends in distant places. The rhymes referred to were poems enclosed in the above note, and not the tail-piece to his letter.

On another occasion, Anderton and a friend accepted an invitation to visit some poor societies in the districts remote from the scenes of their usual advocacy. The journey, including the time for holding the meetings, took nearly three weeks. Every inch of the ground was travelled on foot, through bad roads, and in snowy weather. Most of the meetings were held in the open air, which seriously affected his health. On returning home, and when more than twenty miles from Preston, his strength failed him, and, to add to the unpleasantness, it was getting dark. This compelled him to abandon the idea of reaching home that night. But there was another difficulty to be overcome, more nipping to his courage than hoar frost. The little "hutch" they had saved for their labour of love was nearly exhausted,—the pockets of both were nearly empty. There was no difference between the two pilgrims, except that the one was better qualified for roughing it. "Now," said Anderton to his friend, "you may do as you like about going home, but out of this place I will not go to night ; I'll dispute possession for a berth with that image in the archway first." At that moment, a fine-looking country woman, in the prime of beauty, was coming towards him. He said, glancing his eyes towards the woman, "that's a rare motherly body ; she will understand what it is to have a lad from home." He spoke to her, telling her who he was, how far he and "that other chap" had been travelling ; what caused him to ramble from home, and what was the matter with him. When he had finished, she exclaimed, "Well, if I ever saw anything like this before in all my born days. It's vast queer that I should come this way to go home ; I was going to take t'other turn, but I could not get on at any rate ; I felt as though I could see a boggart i'th road. I know what it was now—I wur to see thee. I am glad, God bless thee ! for thou art a gradely good 'un. My lasses, in Preston, sent us word many a time about thee, and one of them is over now, Christmassing. She will be reet glad to see thee, and that other chap,— what did'st call him ?" What a glorious nature is woman's ! The kind look, the sweet tones of the voice of this charming woman banished pain and trouble from the weary travellers. Arrived at her cottage, the daughter rushed out, and exclaimed, "Well, I declare, if here is'nt Henry Anderton," and flying to him, as though he had been her sweetheart, she said, "but I am some fain to see thee, Henry." The night was spent in talking about the events of the journey, and he ever after spoke of it as one of the happiest of his life. His speech in the Cockpit, descriptive of this journey, was, perhaps, never equalled by himself, for beauty and pathos. The genius of Anderton was kept alive as much by the enthusiasm it created in others, as by its own inherent strength.

When we survey the situation and circumstances of the early advocates, we find their duties and comforts altogether different to anything now existing. The difficulties they had to contend against, demanded unremitting activity, and the brutal opposition by which they were assailed, required the most vigorous exertion to overcome it. Those common enjoyments, which unite and foster the ties of friendship, were put beyond their reach. In this state of things, the allurements of ease or peace could no more charm them than the inhabitants of the desert, and yet, great as the discouragements were, the progress of the cause was as much accelerated by the opposition of its enemies as the zealous and disinterested efforts of its friends. It is a duty to remind those who sometimes condescend to allude to the Preston men, that there is nothing in the present state of things that resembles, in the least particular, the times when Anderton laboured for the cause. The word advocate then did not denote what the word signifies at present. In the Preston sense, that term applied to every one who maintained the doctrine of total abstinence ; the advocacy had not then become a profession. In this general sense, there were many of the rough-and-ready class, but, even in its most restricted meaning, there were no men who subsisted by their own advocacy. The Preston men gave their time, and spent their own money ; they entered towns and villages without invitation, made their speeches, and scattered their tracts by the way. For a long time, they kept alive what they had created at home and in other places. The Preston society was not established for the support of its advocates, but the cause ; the society did not create them, but they created the society. There never was an institution in modern times like that original and brave confederacy. There was no unmerited preference given,—the motive power to mischief was excluded from their noble design. Every one, from the least to the greatest, was ready for his work according to his ability. Those whose talents gave them the highest place in public esteem, made no sport of their humble brethren. Preston did not derive its men, any more than its means, from other places,—they had a man for every kind of work, and fit for home or foreign service. They were the best men I have ever known in the cause ; their loyalty to truth and to each other was worthy the age of heroes ; they were above fear, and, therefore, dreaded no man ; like good men who knew their duty, they did it without regard to consequences. They had less talk and more work than falls to the lot of some folk now-a-days, but what they said would "bide the reckoning." Good officers make good soldiers ; here is the rule of our ancient constitution relating to our commanding officers :—

(2.) "The affairs of the society shall be managed by a committee, consisting of treasurer, secretary, captains, and others, who shall meet as often as it may be deemed necessary for the transaction of business, nine of whom shall form a quorum."

It will sometimes happen that people unfit for the service get into the ranks, —the following was the rule relating to the "flat-footed" gentlemen who loitered behind :—

(3.) "In cases of delinquency, the members shall be visited by one or more of the committee, and, if deemed irreclaimable, expelled by them. The expulsion may be read up at the next public meeting."

I need not ask how many of the existing temperance societies have rules like the foregoing ; or how many committee-men undertake such delicate duties as were assigned to them in the third. From what has been stated, it will appear evident that, during the time the Preston Society maintained its separate and independent action, there were no agency arrangements in existence, consequently, neither Anderton nor any other person was an advocate, as the term is used now. I am the more anxious in stating these particulars now, than I should feel myself called upon to do at any other time, by a sense of its importance, that I may guard the reader against forming wrong ideas as to Anderton's want of employment. What happened in his case may have happened to others, in fact, did, to some extent. The blow that struck him down came from the club of the publicans; the temperance men could not avert that blow, but his friends did what they could to heal the wound, and lessen his troubles. There is another thing I wish to remark, by way of caution, namely this, when I use a term denoting the absence of riches among these early temperance men, I do not mean that they were poor in the vulgar sense. They had nothing but what they earned by their labour, but they were richer and more independent than any advocates that have appeared since. Anderton then was not an advocate, except in the same sense as all the rest of the members were. The term was never applied to him; he was called "the orator" and "the poet" of the movement, and his title remains undisputed to the present hour. He was of more consequence than all the other Preston men put together, and, in saying this, I defraud no man of his honours. The publicans, therefore, judged well, when they concluded if they could silence his saucy muse they could easily silence the rest. How they succeeded in their intent, this collection of his poems will show.

An impudent temperance official, who has since died a drunkard, wrote to a friend of the poet's a letter about his politics and religion. As the names of many persons yet living are given in Anderton's reply, I shall give only a short extract:—

"I see by the remarks at the close of your letter to ——, that that common-liar, Report, has made you believe that I am a Turn-coat and a Tory. I had the misfortune to be popular with the people; Envy caught hold of my independent, anti-party politics to pull down my fame, and build up her own; but that was a work not within her grasp. The people knew me too well, and trust me too confidently 'to be blown about with every wind of doctrine'; and to prove that this is the case, I need only add, that a distinguished Christian Radical has just made me a present of a beautiful Bible. I never was more popular than I am now with the teetotallers and the inhabitants of 'Proud Preston.' So much for what other folk think; and now for a little insight into my own imaginings. I am, sir, what I always was—the friend of universal freedom, and, especially, the civil emancipation of the working classes. To secure them this liberty, I would give every man, of sound mind and good morals, a vote. I would protect that vote by the ballot, and to keep corruption from the Senate, our representatives should be elected every year. These principles may be hated, and those who maintain them persecuted by such reformers as ——, and every dirty, grasping, hypocritical, yes-and-no scoundrel in the service of ——; yet, Radical as I am in civil matters, I have some queer notions about religion. I never was, and I never will be, the tool of any faction. I will go with any one as far as conscience will accompany me, but not a step beyond, to obtain a crown. But I have another reason for disliking, for hating, the Radicalism of the present day. Its principal champions are infidels. You know how much these Radicals talk about the 'march of intellect,' and the 'diffusion of knowledge,' and what effect it must have upon the public mind. You know what they say ; but, have you watched its progress and marked its tendencies ? Look at your political Goliaths—Hetherington, Cleave, Owen, and Carlile ; men who call the Bible priest-craft, and religion cant. Do you think that the blessing of God will hallow a cause whose advocates dispute his word and doubt his being ? 'Them that honor me, saith the Lord, I will honor.' But, these Radicals of our day, despise and insult Him, and on that ground I have come out from amongst them."

The position he had taken brought him to a dead stand, and he resolved to retire from public life rather than expose himself to the annoyance of designing and selfish officials.

The letter to the officials is very characteristic, and calls to mind some circumstances Preston men will understand without more specific allusion. See how pointedly he alludes to the gift of his "Christian Radical." He received another gift, which may be mentioned to the honour of those who gave it. It was a silver star, which he always wore at his breast on great occasions. This present was intended to symbolize his rank in the class of public men at that time acknowledged as speakers on the temperance question. The present was made at Hulme, August 6th, 1836, Mr. James Gaskill in the chair. There was a brilliant gathering on the occasion, and he made a noble speech later on, but said little when the present was given to him. These were his words on receiving the gift :—

"Ladies and Gentlemen,—It gives me great pleasure to be with you once more, especially under circumstances like the one which has brought us together this day; you to give me a token of your continued good will, and I to receive that expression of kindness at your hands. In accepting this beautiful present, you must not expect from me a long and laboured speech about the thrilling sensations which crowd into my mind, and deprive me of the power of uttering my gratitude for your unexpected and undeserved favour, as some mountebank speechifyers would do.

"Ladies and Gentlemen,—I have yet to learn how to administer the unction of flattery to the vanity of man, at the expense of truth. Neither was I much surprised when I first heard of your kind intentions towards your humble servant.

"I did not expect this, certainly; but I knew, by some chance means or other, I had won your esteem. I know that love, when well grounded, will speak out, and give 'outward and visible signs' of attachment to the object so beloved,—and thus you show your love to me. Yet, though I was not much surprised, your favour is not the less welcome. I am poor, and, therefore, your motive in bestowing it was disinterested and pure; and, because I believe them to be such, allow me to say that this substantial proof of your kindness shall never depart from my keeping, and while I travel through this 'vale of tears,' I will stow the remembrance of your kindness in my heart. Yes, ladies and gentlemen, I can be grateful ; 'tis true I cannot show it as you have done to me; that would require money,—and, like Peter the Apostle, 'silver and gold have I none.' But in heart work I shall prove your match, and the future shall convince you that I can return your kindness, and love for love.

> " 'Tis an exquisite keepsake, a beautiful present ;
> And this is the chain, whose bright links are to bind
> Our souls in a bond,—not like dew evanescent,
> But like what it is, of a durable kind ;
> Aye, lasting as life, for I utter no fib here,
> Nor shall your kind gift from my keeping depart,
> 'I'll stow it,' as Jack says, beneath the fifth rib here,
> And there I will wear it—next door to my heart."

This address is a confirmation of what 1 have stated respecting his circumstances,—not for a few days or weeks, but for years. He incidently takes the opportunity to teach the people a great lesson. First, that there is nothing shameful in honest poverty ; and, secondly, that a poor man need not disgrace himself by becoming a sycophant. Then mark how he tests the purity of motive in the givers,—he is poor, and cannot return the gift in kind, hence there is no ground for suspicion.

I fear it will not appear quite satisfactory to some that Anderton was not known as a worker in the cause beyond the first period. I do not feel myself obliged to say much by way of accounting for his retirement from a work for which he was so well qualified, though much might easily be said upon that point. In addition to what he hints at in his note to the " official," I have added the explanation. A change began about this time in the mode of carrying on the work. Many societies had been established in various places, and, notwithstanding most were in a flourishing state, no advocates had appeared able to defend the cause with adequate efficiency in any of these separate societies. This fact ought to claim attention, and stimulate our historical gentlemen to ascertain the cause. I am familiar with the evasion substituted in the place of the genuine explanation,—the old cry of novelty is always at hand to hide the nakedness of the land. But the old fashioned talk about the novelty having worn away, will not account for the fact stated. It is quite certain that the novelty of the movement did not gain it acceptance at the first, and surely it was more novel then than at any other time. But those who took part in the advocacy at the date referred to, know that no men ever obtained a position by more determined efforts than the Preston men obtained theirs. Novelty was no help, but a hindrance, the imputation of which was one of the charges they had to refute. That the cause in Preston was unpopular needs no proof. The violent character of the opposition was not confined to words, misrepresentation and detraction were often the provocatives to greater indignities; yet, in spite of these, and without help from others, they not only established their own cause upon a solid basis, but won for themselves a reputation for eloquence, which none before or since have been able to realize. They maintained what they had won. Their popularity was not made by the puffing system ; the press did nothing for them ; they earned it by the only means that ought to secure it to any one—merit. The "unction of flattery," to use the expression of our poet, was never administered to any one by them, even in "cases of extreme necessity." So stingy of praise are our publications of this period, that we often fail to squeeze out of them even the name of the speakers whose labours are recorded. They were not indebted to the partiality of their fellow citizens for their exclusive pre-eminence. In town or village, however remote from home, the same estimation was formed of their abilities. The attendance at the Cock-pit, from the first year to the last of their appearance, was as great, and the enthusiasm as intense, as it had ever been known. Nothing, ever seen in England, equalled these famous meetings, which proves that these old advocates were masters of their situation. Now, it is a matter of experience that no one can deny, that the societies which sprang up in other places, when they began to act for themselves, never did create out of their own body a class of men that could do for their societies what is admitted, on all hands, the Preston men did for theirs. But I may venture to make the statement more positive by asserting that even the Preston men themselves have never been able to create successors to their old advocates. The town stands were it did ; some portions of that noble army I knew in my youth are still there,—Mr. Livesey is yet living ; he remembers the times and the men I am speaking about,—and I appeal to them whether the glory of those days has been repeated.

To remedy the defect arising from the deficiency of local talent, and in some measure to meet the growing demand for assistance, a plan was devised of uniting the separate societies into one association. At this point the original temperance movement ceased, and a new order of things commenced. The old broad principles of the first period began to disappear, and the old defenders of these principles were neglected and despised. The change was so rapid, the results so disasterous, that fear and dismay spread through our ranks like a panic. The experience gained ought to have taught others beside the Preston men the vast importance of a good constitution and a good committee, for much of the renown of the Preston Society may be traced to these two particulars. The talents necessary for official acts are very different to those required in a skilful advocate. They should be competent to estimate the character and ability of those who push themselves forward as advocates, for, since they are not able to do everything which ought to be accomplished by their own abilities, the least that can be required of them is, that they are honest enough to apply the talents of others. I have said that the Preston Society could find a man for everything they had to do, but of what advantage would that have been, had there been no heads to know the nature of the work to be done, and the man who could do it ?

It is hardly necessary to show that a departure from the "old plan" was followed by a change of doctrine and discipline ; these things shall be fully and satisfactorily shown on some future occasion. Without attempting, therefore, to illustrate a fact well-known to the old reformers, it will, I imagine, excite some surprise now, as it did to some Preston men at the time, that at the moment these new arrangements were being made, Anderton and all the other Preston men were overlooked. That fact will have to be accounted for some day, and many others that seem to have slipped from the memory of our history makers. Anderton's letter to the "official," and the speech on receiving the gift of his friends in Hulme, not only furnish a glimpse of his own splendid character, but, indirectly, of that vanity and vice, which, for the first time, made its appearance in our midst. This was the time when merit was neglected, and ignorance and folly strutted in the robes of office over despised genius and virtue, and the country was overrun with a pampered crew of sensualists, idiots, and hypocrites. The evil became so general and appalling as to fill our minds with the dismal apprehension of annihilation. The Preston men still retained, to some extent, the authority of their old name, and once more took their position in the front ranks to repel this invasion of the Goths. The echo of their war cry came over the hills and sounded in the valleys, and Nantwich, Chester, Liverpool, and the Isle of Man, joined the glorious old warriors against the traitors. The following extract from a letter written at this time will enable those who are young in the faith to comprehend how these things were managed :—

* * * * "Bids me tell you confidentially that he is not satisfied with the things going on at head quarters. He looks with suspicion at the number of persons, who, unable to get engagements, have, to obtain a popularity talent would never have secured them, joined our ranks, and elbowed themselves into office:—Our advocates, too, when in country places, put ' Rev.' to their names, which I fear is injudicious. The day is gone by when that title appended to a man's name was a sort of talisman that enthroned him in people's hearts and confidence. The world understands genuine Christianity too well now, to be the dupes of would-be priests, and the great moral reform our advocates are endeavouring to effect will progress all the better for being, and appearing, free from the tendency which has been proved inimical to the religion it was meant to serve."

When the people had examined the root of the mischief, and had time to look about them, they began to make inquiry after their old friend Anderton. A warm-hearted woman, who had been his friend and physician, in an illness brought on by anxiety and trials, was the first who made the attempt to induce him to appear again in the defence of the old principles: But she was too late, for before her letter reached him he had taken his final leave of the platform. In his reply to her, he said, "I am quite tied to my desk ; and, if not, I am so sick of exposing myself in public, that you will never hear of my speaking for ' the term of my natural life.' " He lost his business; gave his talents and all he had to the cause ; but he never deserted nor lost a friend. He continued to remember them in his retirement, and wrote pieces for them and their children. His heart was with us still, and his prayers went daily to heaven for our protection and success. Every fresh trouble that afflicted his old companions hurt him as though it had fallen upon himself. When death took any away, he wept with those that were left behind. His motives were pure and his life virtuous. No one had such unlimited confidence placed in them as had Anderton,—the old women told him their troubles, and the young ones their disappointments.

The following letter to a friend, respecting the printing of one of his poems, will show his painstaking to do the smallest thing he undertook well :—

" Dear ————,—The song should be headed ' The Robber, Liar, and Quack,' so you will please have ' Quack' inserted instead of 'Thief.' Walker's Dictionary gives patronise with ' s,' and Johnson with ' z,' but as Walker is more modern, you had better have it spelt 'patronise.' The word ' cosey' or 'cozy' is a flash term, in no dictionary but Pearce Egan's, but I think the former is the proper way of spelling it,—this as you think proper. In verse nine there is an error which spoils the rhyme,—for 'vats' is no rhyme to 'notes.' Let that part of the verse stand thus, as daddy Dunn says :—

> "'The tavern knaves would cease to thrive
> On folly's spongy throats,
> Or spin, from our elastic guts,
> His rolls of five pound notes.'

"I find I have given an incorrect reading of Cowper, for the motto,—it ought to be as follows :—

> —— "'Obey th' important call !
> Her cause demands th' assistance of your throats ;
> Ye all can swallow, and she asks no more.'

Pray, let this be attended to, for quotations should be made correctly. There is one other small alteration, it is in the last verse but one,—'The choicest bits' is written in italics, the three words should be printed in the regular type, and 'choicest bits' as a quotation.

"Will you be kind enough to tell the printer to take off the border ; it looks so much like a 'last dying speech and confession' concern. If he could put a plain double or single line round, with no ornament at the corners, it would look much better.

"I am sorry to give you so much trouble ; but, for 'Auld Lang Syne's sake,' I know the work will be to you a 'labour of love.' As there is nothing to shame one in the ditty, you may print my full name at the bottom, leaving out Fleetwood, of course. I have enclosed 5s., which will pay for two hundred. I cannot afford to pay for more out of my own pocket, and I have written it chiefly to warm the cockles of the hearts of the Rechabites of Fleetwood. If you think it would do any good amongst your good men and true, you may spread abroad to the right and to the left ; two hundred will cost four shillings and ninepence ; the extra threepence will cover your expense of paper, envelope, and postage stamps. A thousand thanks for your care in correcting the press, and I am, yours truly,   "HENRY ANDERTON.

"You will think this miserably written for a clerk, but I have just recovered from a severe indisposition.

"Let the song be printed on the better paper."

He became an agent for the Preston and Wyre Railway Company in the year 1840, and during his residence at Fleetwood, he occasionally spoke at some of the temperance and religious festivals. In 1847 he removed to Heywood, and in the following year to Bury, as agent to the Lancashire and Yorkshire Railway Company, where he continued till his death, which took place June 21st, 1855, in the forty-seventh year of his age.

ANDERTON'S POEMS.

A PEEP INTO THE TAP-ROOM, AND ITS
VISITORS.

While follies abound and Drunkards are found,
  Can pity and scorn remain neuter?
Our tongues shall break loose, at the pitiful goose
  Who glories in handling the "pewter!"
The wretch has down-trod the image of God
  And sunk it below the brute level;—
As much like a man as chaff is like bran;
  He looks and he acts like the Devil!

We'll just have a quiz, at the sot as he is,
  The moral "black cattle" he herds with,
As seated in rows, like strings of scarecrows,
  Which husbandmen frighten the birds with.
You enter the room, and snuff a perfume,
  Compared with which essence so frightful;
Bone-dust is a treat, guano is sweet,
  And garbage extremely delightful!

We've stood at the door, ten minutes or more
  The swine have done nothing but guzzle;
Each covered with stripes of "bacco" and swipes,
  From his gooseberry eyes to his muzzle.
That bloated old prig has dropped like a pig,
  And in the rank puddle he wallows;
His crony still up, with snout in the cup,
  Alternately vomits and swallows!

With long snarling face, and awful grimace,
   There growls a political patriot ;
Yon brace with black eyes, and lips of such size
   Are " good uns"—at tapping the claret!
Those scheming old rooks, in opposite nooks,
   Fresh tricks with dice-box are playing;
That wild-looking youth is " spouting" forsooth,
   And rivals the jackass in braying!

A couple of bores are down on all fours,
   Each other most ruefully eyeing ;
They swear to be trumps, the precious old frumps,
   And finish by hugging and crying !
Yon spectre so grim, with eye glazed dim,
   Death grins at yon perishing noddy ;
His limbs bend and shake ; the worms will soon make
   A jolly good feast on his body !

The rest are mere mutes, poor common place brutes—
   Suspicion itself cannot wrong them;
A fourpenny bit will break the whole kit—
   You cannot raise twopence among them !
This addle-brain'd throng roars out for a song ;
   " Jim Crow" is the idol they stick up ;
When, mad as March hares, pipes, glasses, and chairs,
   Are smash'd in the shindy they kick up.

What squabbles and fights, what stomach pump sights,
   Assail the astonish'd spectator ;
His nose takes offence, and faintings commence,
   If there he remain any later !
What litter and spew, what a horrible crew,
   Delirium destroying their features ;
What lunatic mirth, what a hell upon earth ;
   And *these* are your rational creatures !

But here's the police—the keeper of peace—
   He bawls through the door " turn those men out ;"
At the word of command mine host waves his hand,
   And waddles to clear his foul den out !

The clock has struck "one," he mutters " Be gone,"
When lo ! what a clamour he raises ;
They call for more tick, but, stiff as a brick,
    He bids them " Go home or to blazes !"

" Go home !" how absurd ! to spend that sweet word
    On four crumbling walls is a mockery !
The " bum" has been there and stripp'd them quite bare,
    " My uncle" has taken the crockery !
In closets below, on trusses of straw,
    Exposed to the wind and the weather,
Enclosed in old rugs, wife, children, and bugs,
    Are lovingly huddled together!

As ragged as a colt, or bird in the moult,
    And lean as a winter cock robin ;
No pan on his hob, no brass in his fob—
    The skulking and penniless gobbin !
His skull a crack'd jar, his brain below par,
    And stunning our ears with the rackets ;
Old Bedlam's the spot fit up for the sot,
    For madmen are best in strait jackets.

—————

IT'S WORTH YOUR WHILE!

Come, drunkards ! we've good news for ye,
    Dispense with that derisive smile, men ;
There's freedom for you,—come and see,
    And try your luck,—it's worth your while, men.

Jerry has made your lookers wink ;
    Ar'nt you a set of precious ninnies,
To let the landlord " fork" your jink,
    That he may " flare up" with the guineas ?

You, and your suction-liking " pals,"
    Have given him wealth, and, with the bonus,
His lady buys her " fal-de rals,"
    And " comes it" like a marchioness.

A 2

And, on his rising, upstart breed
    Your hard-won, ill-spent brass, displayed is—
The proud son " mounts his gallant steed"—
    The jewell'd daughters dash like ladies.

And with your " threepencies," for which
    You drain his slop-containing chalice,
The brigand goes to pasture, rich
    As Nabob, to his country palace !

And, worst of all, you're in his debt,
    For in his black book there's an entry,
For shots unsettled, which, to get,
    He hands the " six and eightpence gentry."

And then you have to run a race
    With Bob, the " bum," that " come and fetch" man,
" My Uncle," with his Hebrew face,
    And Maister " What's your will ?," the Scotchman.

My eyes ! but you may well look glum,
    Your ribs so bare, your cheeks so bony,
Worried by landlord, shark, and " bum,"
    And " twa for one " exacting Sawney.

It's worth your while to turn this scale,
    With resolution, firm as Cato's,
To give this pack of wolves " leg bail,"
    And make them work for their potatoes.

It's worth your while, my lads, if you
    Some good fat beef your ribs would toss in,
And cease to glut those lubbers, who,
    As Tummus says, " Are welly brossen" !

It's worth your while, my lads, to hush
    Their daughters' sneers, their ladies' snarlings,
The tears from your wife's eyes to brush,
    And clothe, like theirs, your own poor darlings.

It's worth your while to save your pence,
    To lay your "spare uns" altogether;
They'll serve you twenty winters hence,
    When age creeps on, and rainy weather.

It's worth your while to make your homes
    By "bums" unstripp'd, by duns unpress'd;
Edens, where discord never comes;
    Snug, cherished, cheerful, pure, and blessed.

Too long you've liked this here brown pap,
    And cried like babbies for your "suckey;"
It's worth your while to "stop that tap,"
    And make Old Jerry "cut his lucky."

Stop it! and give "Old Nick" the sulks;
    Make Tom-and-Jerry's bulwarks rock again;
Drive to their spades his bull-neck'd hulks;
    And make the Sawney tribe "gang bock again."

TO THE DRUNKEN POLITICIAN.

Ye champions of freedom, oppression's out-wormers,
    Who would roast every tyrant on liberty's spit,
Ye air-castle stormers, ye dram shop reformers,
    "Give ear," for I want to "chop logic" a bit.

Political drunkards are all "losing stakes" men,
    Who take *losing* methods to get what each craves;
You're poor as March rabbits, and poverty makes men
    What drunkards deserve to be, Paupers and Slaves!

One talks of "repealing the taxes on knowledge,"
    Sufficiently loud "the deaf adder" to vex;
Yet he must have been taught at a learn-nothing college,
    For the gobbin can't tell a big Q from an X.

And one, because some "turn their coats," keeps a-mourning,
   And if he could catch 'em, the scamps he would "muz";
Yet, I think in my heart he had better be turning
   His *own*, for it cannot *look worse than it does.*

Another would "wipe off our national debt," and
   He'd dot with the "sponge" of which Cobbett could talk,
Yet to wipe off his own "debt" a sponge he can't get, and
   He still is the dupe of the *two-for-one* chalk.

Another would get out of tyranny's books, but
   He's down in his grocer's, who gives him a squeeze,
For he gets not a penny, by hook or by crook, but
   Goes *there* for "trust" bacon, and maggotty cheese!

Another would make "freedom get on her legs," but
   His thoughts must be rank "topsy-turvyish" grown;
He might doctor poor liberty's "shish-shashle" pegs, but
   The sot has quite lost the use of his own.

One will never *desert* those who live by their labours,
   "The struggle with him will but end with his life,"
Yet the wretch (and it's very well known to his neighbours)
   Has been "cribbed," above once, for "deserting his wife!"

Another would "kindle a radical bonfire,"
   To burn up the trash and the dross of the state,
Yet for one week, at least, he has never had one fire,
   To warm his blue nose in his own rusty grate!

Another would "patch up our laws," and he itches
   To mend 'em wherever a rent place appears;
Yet he can't pay his tailor for mending his breeches;
   Just look! what a couple of leg sleeves he wears.

Another would "loose all the slaves in the nation,"
   And till he has loos'd 'em he never would stop;
Yet, he must have glanced o'er his own situation,
   For the fellow can't loose his own shirt out of pop.

When election time comes, these men chatter like parrots,
  And if bawling would win, then would tyranny fall;
But they live in unregistered cellars and garrets,
  And, having no votes, they are nothing at all.

Are you blind, or aught worse, drunken champions of free-
    dom?
Hear me out, I beseech you, I know what you'd say;
You would give their full rights to the millions who need 'em ;
  " Amen" ! I reply, but you go the wrong way.

We've had talkings sufficient, and now we want actions ;
  Your cups have undone you, lay these on the shelves;
Leave the shell of reform unto parties and factions;
  Seize the kernel at once by reforming yourselves.

Let our Joiners and Spinners, Mechanics and Founders,
  Keep the brass they once spent on their bowls in their fists ;
Their money thus saved, what a crowd of *ten pounders*
  Might rally round Freedom, and swell out her lists!

Teetotal's your engine ; it looks but a puny one ;
  But, work it,—you'll find it gives strength to the weak,
For, thus knit, we shall form a Political Union,
  Which tyrants may hack at, but never can break.

TO DRUNKARDS.

Irrational beings! your senseless career
  Will speedily lead you to misery's brink ;
And yet, ye rush onward, untortur'd by fear,
  Nor pause on the threshold of hell, ere you sink.

Forsake, oh! forsake the foul paths you have trod ;
  Repent in the dust, or be fearfully driven
From Hope, and the smiles of a merciful God,
  And lost to the consummate glories of heaven.

Ye rush to the tomb, unredeem'd, unprepar'd,
   With God for your firm and inflexible foe ;
And hell is the pardonless sinner's reward,
   And thither the unreclaim'd drunkard must go.

Yet Jesus invites you ; his messenger waits
   To carry your tardy repentance on high :
Oh ! sue for a passport through Salem's bright gates,
   And " cease to do evil"—" for why will you die ?"

The pleasures of drunkenness cannot repay
   The hearts she has stabb'd to the innermost core,
Nor her peril-fraught brimmers of death charm away
   The fire she infuses through every pore.

This vice is the parent of fear and remorse,
   And madness and ruin, and shame and despair,
Which brand on the heart an indelible curse,
   A venom which bubbles eternally there.

If Zion has beauties to draw your desires,
   Why, why do you run in an opposite path ?
If hell's unconceiv'd and unquenchable fires
   Affright you, why waken God's measureless wrath ?

I command, I entreat, I implore you, by all
   Heaven's infinite joy and hell's terrible pain,
This moment emerge from the drunkard's dark thrall,
   And wake to the sunshine of Mercy again.

THE JOYS OF DRINKING.

What are the drunkard's boasted hopes
   Which his besotted soul relies on ?
For surely they are falling props,
   If they are bas'd on drinking poison.

Tell me what joys a man can own
  Who spends his leisure on the bottle,
And pours fermented liquors down
  His satisfied, unthirsting "throttle."

Drink may, it does, its dupes beguile
  From toil, or care, or pain, or sorrow;
And thus it will bewitch them, while
  Those dupes can beg, or steal, or borrow;
But when resources fail, oh! then
  Listen the sighs the drunkard "fetches;"
The after-clap is unmixed pain,
  The sot a wretch above all wretches!

And drink exhilirates the man
  While it exists within the body,
But when its fumes approach the brain,
  It makes that man a senseless noddy;
And drinking is the soul of fun,
  And jollity, and wit, and laughter;
But soon as these effects are gone,
  It makes him smell of hell fire after!

Yon public-house looks snug and neat,
  But how can landlords bait that hook so?
Sots help those robbers to complete
  That snugness, and to make them look so.
They rob their own domestic cots
  Of joy and comfort which adorn them,
And part with independent lots
  To fatten publicans who scorn them!

The drunkard fills the landlord's purse,
  And clothes their haughty, purse-proud wives too;
And (this is positive and terse)
  He makes them easy all their lives too.
But where's his wife?—his children, where?
  He knows not—recks not—what they're doing;
Dead to their accents of despair,
  And callous to their utter ruin!

Hell gapes for him—oh! strive to win
   The drunkard from a state so awful!
Reclaim him from this frightful sin;
   Snatch—pluck him from a fate so woeful!
God of the world! prepare our way,
   Forgive the drunkard's oft-rebellings,
Resume thy sovereign moral sway,
   And drive the monster from our dwellings.

THE PURGE.

Said a man to the "gemman" who told us the tale,
"You may say what you list against drinking 'good ale;'
Your efforts are vain, and 'tis bootless to urge,
For still I think ale is an excellent purge."

"You are right," quoth my friend, "'tis a purge sure
     enough,
Let the penniless pockets of drunkards give proof;
It makes them to vomit their 'silver' and 'brass,'
And he who denies it's a genuine ass.

Not only does ale purge its swillers from wealth,
It purges a man from contentment and health;
Pray look at the drunkard! his visage so blue
Proclaims that his dose was unerringly true!

'Tis a purge from the boasted enjoyments of life;
Look! look at the drunkard's poor children and wife!
His offspring's wan looks, and his wife's startled throes,
Evince that the purge is too powerful—God knows!

It purges its patient from freedom; nowhere
Is this purge so incredibly potent as there;
It makes the poor slave (the sheer wisdomless elf)
In love with the chains of the Devil himself!

It purges from life—and oh ! there is its sting ;
How many poor souls has it forced to take wing ?
And where could they fly to ?   Where sinners must go
That die unredeem'd, and with God for their foe !

A purge ?   To be sure 'tis an excellent purge,
But is it not also the deadliest scourge
That ever laid man so successfully low,
Or spread lamentation, and wailing, and woe ?"

Sobriety ! come, with thy health-mantled brow,
Counteract this vile purge with pure abstinence now ;
Thine advocates bless, and thy children inspire
With some of thy god-like, benevolent fire.

God ! rouse thy faint-hearted disciples at length,
Supply us with wisdom and sin-scourging strength,
And grant that this pest may be banish'd and hurl'd
From our circles, our country, our homes, and the world.

UP, AND BE DOING, LADS.

Tune—" God save the Queen."

What though these topers all,
Madmen and mopers, all
    Make such a fuss ;
It is all vanity,
Drunken insanity :—
Friends of humanity !
    God is with us !

We shall not totter yet,
Though they wax hotter yet,
    Demon and man ;
Though they surround us now
'Twould not astound us now ;
They can't confound us now—
    God leads our van !

Drugs we have swill'd enow,
Men they have kill'd enow,
          Quit yourselves well :
"Up, and be doing," lads !
Stop all this brewing, lads,
Till this wide ruin, lads,
          Settles in hell.

Zion's true soldiers, come !
Reason upholders, come !
          Fear not nor shrink.
Fight till these dandy shops—
Rum, gin, and brandy shops—
Beelzebub's handy shops—
          Shut up or sink !

————

TOPERS AND MOPERS.

Are not topers hood-wink'd mopers,
          Through this vale of tears,
Growing madder, growing sadder,
          As they grow in years ?

Are not drinkers daily sinkers
          In the mire of sin ?
What's undone them ?—Out upon them,
          Brandy, rum, and gin.

Lo ! the swiller !   The self-killer !
          Where can reason be ?
Drink o'erthrew it, and he knew it—
          What a wretch is he !

When a fellow gets "right mellow,"
          Turn your eyes that way ;
See him "pick-up !" hear him hiccup !
          Hark his ass-like bray !

With their wives all—woe survives all—
Death steals on a-pace ;
Sorrow's traces on their faces
Wither every grace !

And their young ones, prattling tongued ones,
Hang the drooping head ;
Curse the father who can rather
Drink than see them fed.

The All-seeing made this being,
Never more to die—
Form'd his spirit to inherit
Bliss beyond the sky !

But can drunken men, so sunken,
Tread this upward path ?
No, they're flying, rushing, hieing,
To eternal wrath !

Hell is watching, arm'd for snatching
Their poor souls away :
Foes of evil, foil the Devil—
Rob him of his prey !

OH! NOW FOR A TUG!

Oh ! now for a tug with the glass and the jug !
Let's arm for the struggle like Turks !
And join in the quarrel with bottle and barrel,
And bung-hole, and vent-pegs, and corks !
Let us fire our "bomb shells," until Beelzebub swells
With anger—the sooty old thief !
Away with their jerry !—and make yourself merry
With ham, and plum-pudding, and beef !
            Give the proud landlords a lash !
            Guzzle no more of their trash !

The landlord's puff'd crew, and the jerry-lords, too,
  We'll make 'em bestir their fat shanks!
Oh! yes, we'll make all, both great ones and small,
  Asham'd of their drug-vending pranks!
Though they swagger so now, we'll take them in tow,
  And clip them before—ay, and aft—
At one mighty swoop we'll level the troop,
  And ruin their villanous craft!
                    Give, &c.

When the trade is all fled, let 'em work for their bread,
  With more honest and likelier tools;
For no longer they'll dine, and grow fat, and look fine,
  With the labour-wrung pennies of fools!
Those fools will grow wise, when we open their eyes
  To the rogueries of ale-selling quacks;
And they'll lay out their jink—where?—where do you
      think?
  On their children's poor bellies and backs!
                    Give, &c.

And their children the while, and their wives shall beguile
  Their labour and toil.   Would not this
Be a beautiful earth, if our dwellings gave birth
  To pictures so teeming with bliss?
" Old Harry" would grin, and death, hell, and sin
  Would mourn their "unmendable" fall.
God help us to fight with these monsters of night,
  And make us triumphant o'er all!
                    Give, &c.

A FAREWELL TO DRUNKENNESS.

Farewell to strong drink, whether spirits or ale!
For me they may dry, or grow sour, or turn stale:
I've done with the bowl, and the midnight carouse,
I'm sick of the maddening and brain-stealing "pouse!"
              Farewell, Jerry! Farewell, Jerry!
              Farewell, Jerry, I'm out of thy books!

Farewell to the sighs of my wife, and the wild
And heart-rending cries of my hunger-wrung child;
They've smiles and affection, they've bed and they've board,
And a home to its drink-driven comforts restored!
Farewell, &c.

Farewell to " my uncle's !"—I've money enough;
My earnings will purchase our "family stuff":
And having no old nor new drink-shots to pay,
The o'erplus I'll save for a slattery day!
Farewell, &c.

Farewell to the dram-store and jerry-shop!—Why?
No more shall their picture-signs dazzle my eye:
My pocket, and conscience, and health are still sore
From the scratches I got at those hell-holes before!
Farewell, &c.

Farewell to the landlord, his lingo and phiz;
His house is hell's church, and the parson he is;
He praises those drugs, which he knows very well
Will ruin the drunkard, and drive him to hell!
Farewell, &c.

Farewell to " blue devils !"—(thank temperance for that);
I've shrunk many a time from these imps of " Old Scrat;"
For oft on a morning succeeding a spree,
These blue-visag'd phantoms have terrified ME.
Farewell, &c.

Farewell to swell'd eye, bloody nose, and black shin!
The sure fruits of swilling rum, jerry, and gin:
I guzzle none now, and my brain-pan's unrack'd,
My lookers unswell'd, and my walkers unblacked!—
Farewell, &c.

Farewell to my rags !—for at one time my coat,
And waistcoat, and breeches no buttons had got;
So I dress'd on a morning with needle and thread,
And doff'd them with scissors when ready for bed.
    Farewell, &c.

Farewell to the Devil, the drug-shop, and all
The things which conniv'd at and hasten'd my fall;
I'll play this black junto a comical trick—
I'll drink Adam's jerry, and baffle " Old Nick !"
    Farewell, &c.

NEVER TOUCH, LADS!

Thou look'st very queer—thou'rt sufficient to scare
 Whoever may see thee, poor fellow!
Thy " smeller" all o'er with red spots so sore,
 Is pimpled, and thy skin is yellow;
Besides thy red snout, thy shoe toes are out;
 Sad places are these "jerry wag" shops;
And thy hat, and thy coat, and thy breeches have got
 To " my uncle's," or some of the rag shops.

What an object drink makes thee! How sadly it shakes
  thee !
 Sot! art thou not tir'd of thy revels?
In fears thou'rt array'd—What makes thee afraid?
 Why, friend, thou hast got the " blue devils!"
The landlord won't thank thee for drinking, but rank thee
 With fools of the veriest class;
While thy " jink" he receives, he " laughs in his sleeves,"
 And calls thee a good-natured ass.

Dost thou know what has levelled, and maul'd, and be-devil'd,
 And made thee the shame of thy race?
The first glass has done it—a murrain upon it!
 Poor drunkard! I pity thy case!

Whenever "Old Nick" wants to play thee a trick,
The *first glass* will greatly assist him:
Oh! do not give in to the "father of sin,"
But, like a true soldier, resist him.

Let it stick in thy head, what friend Pollard once said—
(For a long-headed fellow he's reckon'd)—
"Don't quaff the first pot, and the Devil can not
Compel you to swallow a second."
Yes, this is the' way to bid him "Good day:"
His drugs we have guzzled too much, lads;
But no longer he'd brag, if we gave him the bag,
And how must we do't?—NEVER TOUCH, LADS!

THE ROBBER, LIAR, AND QUACK,

AS PATRONISED BY LAW.

"Obey your country's call,—
Her cause demands the assistance of your throats;
Ye all can swallow, and she asks no more."—Cowper.

I wonder if these landlords
    Hope to die in their own beds;—
I wonder how such precious scamps
    Can raise their guilty heads;—
I wonder how such "righteous laws"
    Can legalise the sale
Of "Mountain Dew," "Jamaica Cream,"
    And sparkling "Nut-brown Ale!"

The landlord argues with himself,
    "While there are fools to swill,
I'll dose them with my devilries;
    If not, my brethren will."
And with this sop to conscience,
    He pursues his baleful task,
A robber sanctioned by the State,
    With "license" for a mask!

B

The landlord cheats throughout the day,
   The felon prigs at night,
The landlord murders gradually,
   The felon stabs outright;
The landlord is the greater pest,
   Yet while he waxes fat,
His brother dances on the air,
   And sports a hemp cravat!

Mine host can tell a pleasant tale,
   And would his dupes persuade
That sleek and hearty all must be
   Who taste his Stock-in-Trade;
And, pointing to his goodly paunch
   His cheeks so plump and flush,
He'll trace their "rise and progress"
   To a bellyful of lush!

Just step within his cosey snug,
   Behold him at his lunch,
How he tucks in the solids,
   Which he qualifies with punch!
Your money bought that fat surloin—
   Yes, yours, you gaping geese!
Which plasters on the glutton's ribs
   A triple coat of grease!

If we might credit Boniface,
   There's virtue in his swipes
For every mortal malady—
   From typhus to the gripes!
Yes, "barley-broth" is sovereign balm
   For bruise, and throb, and smart,—
There's convalescence in a pint,
   And rapture in a quart!

Behold yon starv'd anatomy,
   Our nature's saddest blot,—
In him your orbs may recognise
   A poor, demented sot!

His rheumy eyes, his wheezing lungs,
  His frame upon the rack;—
These are thy work, oh! man of "drops,"
  Thou unexampled quack!

Experience damns the loathsome craft,
  And frantic nature storms
At the dark frauds man practices
  Upon his fellow worms;
Yet, what avail a nation's cries,
  The prayers of high and low?
The "tap" brings grist to government,
  And tapsters rob by law!

A curse on these decoctions!
  If the sot would close his lips,
The tavern's bad prosperity
  Would undergo eclipse;—
The tavern knave would cease to thrive
  On folly's spongy throats,
Or spin from our elastic guts
  His rolls of five pound notes!

My spleen boils over when I think
  What noodles fuddlers are!
Behold the landlord's ladybird,
  The Empress of the Bar!—
To buy a brooch for that fat neck
  Which swells with vulgar pride,
The sot has pinched his own poor wife,
  His once exulting bride!

Return to us—once more return—
  Insulted common sense!
Let tavern hogs grow fat no more
  At better men's expense;
No more let tyrant appetite
  Make havoc of our wits,—
Make butchers' shops the fashion,
  And give us the "choicest bits."

Back to thy vaults, John Barleycorn!
　A day is coming on
When fools shall learn to save their tin,
　And cherish " number one";
When every sturdy artisan,
　As on he blithely jogs,
Shall follow Shakespeare's maxim—
　And " throw physic to the dogs."

TRY, LADS, TRY.

I have ventured out again,
From my cottage on the plain,
And despite of toil and pain,—
　　　　Hope in view.

I have come to take your part
'Gainst the tempter's wily art;
Drunkards! let us make a start—
　　　　Do, lads, do!

It is in the drunkard's power
To be rescued any hour,
Though the clouds of danger lour
　　　　Thick and near.

Let him " bag" his jerry pots,
Let him shun the place of sots,
Drunkards! if you'd mend your lots,
　　　　Hear, lads, hear.

See the landlord! he can thrive,
While with poverty you strive;
When you sigh—" Dear heart alive,"
　　　　Watch him pass.

Nodding at you all the while,
In a Jack-and-Joan like style,
What's the meaning of his smile ?
      Brass, lads, brass !

Yes, he wants your brass, indeed ;
" Love myself," aye, that's his creed,
When the rascal means to feed
      On your pelf.

Drunkards ! do as he has done,
Keep an eye to number one,
Let your thoughts be turned upon
      Self, lads, self.

When will English dwellings be
Edens of felicity ?
When will English workmen see
      As wise men ?

When will truth and common sense
Prove Old England's best defence ?
When strong drink is banished hence,
      Then lads, then.

It's as easy as " come out"
To bring this nice change about,
If you'd lay these " good for nought"
      Liquids by.

If, instead of jerry dregs,
You would let roast beef and eggs
Occupy your munching pegs :
      Try, lads, try.

GOOD NEWS.

The landlords of Bacup, a short time ago,
Thought to down with our cause with a finishing blow;
And this is the way they began the alarm—
"If you won't drink our ale, you shall not have our barm."

"What a hobble they're in," said these scamps in their souls,
And they made the town ring with their hisses and howls,
As if they could bring irretrievable harm
To our good cause, by shouting, "You shall have no barm."

What narrow-soul'd fellows these landlords must be;
Our Pledge we admire, and our lads would agree
To fight in our ranks,—heart with heart, arm to arm—
Though they forc'd us to live upon bread without barm.

But let these fat-bellied imposters give ear,
Their threat is deserving of naught but a sneer;
We tell the swell'd, lazy, and bitter-tongued elves,
Our chaps will have barm, for WE MAKE IT OURSELVES!

Remove an effect by removing the cause,
That's the rock upon which we have founded our laws;
And therefore, if drunkards are made by strong drink,
Our Pledge is the offspring of Reason, I think.

Then—barm or no barm—I may venture to say,
The trade of the landlord shall dwindle away;
And before we have done—without asking—we'll crack
Our teetotal whip on his very broad back!

Do ye hear what we say, ye brave lads of our town?
Let us bring Jerry-wag and old Beelzebub down;
Let's save the poor drunkard, by hook or by crook,
And stop him from going to "Mitchell-field-Nook."*

---

* The workhouse for Bacup and Newchurch townships.

THE LADS OF BACUP.

What loggerheads these drunkards are,
  The mortal foes of empty glasses;
Their reason hardly on a par
  With geese, and pigs, and sheep, and asses;
Drinking "brown stout" to make 'em strong,
  Which knocks 'em down, and makes 'em take up
Their this side—that side way, along
  The far-too-narrow streets of Bacup.

Strong ale, indeed! yes, strong enough;
  Too strong, by far, for those who venture
To cram their muzzles with such stuff;
  It knocks a fellow off his centre!
'Tis true, about his strength he raves,
  Yet in this village I could rake up
A host of strengthless, helpless slaves,
  Who crowd the jerry-shops of Bacup.

For this the drunkard wastes his time,
  And spends his " coppers" and his " shillings,"
And taints his soul with deepest crime,
  And dines, too oft, on murphy pillings!
For this he plagues his partner's life;
  " Pops" his best coat, that he may make up
A present for the landlord's wife;—
  This is not "jannock," lads of Bacup!

Where, drunkard, dost thou put thy eyes?
  The landlord's rich, and thou art poor, lad;
Learn from this lesson to be wise,
  And darken not his open door, lad!
Thy body is a total wreck;
  I come, thy energies to wake up.
Abstain! for that's the way to check
  The purse-proud jerry-lords of Bacup.

Our plan of cure is prompt and brief—
   Heed not the landlord's hollow proffers ;
Turn o'er another, better leaf,
   Put your own " brass" in your own coffers :
Look closer after " number one :"
   Your dry bones from this slumber shake up ;
The landlords may not like such fun,
   But never mind 'em, lads of Bacup.

Jerry can't " stick," lads, " in your ribs,"
   (Though 'tis the drunkard's darling pet stuff,)
And they can mouth uncommon fibs,
   Who say that drunkards feed on wet stuff ;
What did God give you teeth for, eh ?
   To drink with ? no, to munch a steak up ;
Then cast the landlord's slops away,
   And stick to solids, lads of Bacup !

A TEMPERANCE ADDRESS DELIVERED AT

FLEETWOOD-ON-WYRE.

A pennyworth's food in a gallon of ale,
And what food there is, is both bitter and stale ;
Yet you pay for this pigmeat and swillings and fire,
Two shillings per gallon at Fleetwood-on-Wyre !

One dose for a chap would be more than enough,
If the Devil himself had not got in the stuff ;
For none but Old Nick and the landlords desire
To gain by your folly at Fleetwood-on-Wyre.

Yet you sots are so keen and so gross is your taste,
Your earnings in Jerry you recklessly waste ;
The brass which your far-away families require,
To make yourselves swill-tubs at Fleetwood-on-Wyre.

Wife and child left at home is a part of your plan,
They "scrat up a living" as well as they can ;
So starv'd in their looks, and so ragged in attire,
You can't for shame bring them to Fleetwood-on-Wyre !

Not only his brass, but his tools and his clothes,
The drunkard will give for a "jolly red nose ;"
George Swallow* can tell all who please to enquire,
The tools he has *swallowed* at Fleetwood-on-Wyre.

Four masons† (who acted in this, like four geese)
Pawn'd their every-day coats for a shilling a-piece,
And work'd (as I'm told by a man who's no liar)
A week without jackets at Fleetwood-on-Wyre.

And when you have done all your money and "strap,"‡
The lawyer is ordered to give you a rap ;
And for every fresh sheet which he draws from his quire,
You pay six-and-eightpence at Fleetwood-on-Wyre !

A week or two after your very last spree,
You got from the Scotchman some blankets and tea ;
And sawney's keen fisted, and never will tire,
To " ca' for his siller" at Fleetwood-on-Wyre !

Now, what do you get for your brass and your pains ?
Destruction of health and confusion of brains :
Knocked down by policemen and trail'd through the mire,
Of which there's quite plenty at Fleetwood-on-Wyre.

Yes, drunkards give all for crack'd skulls and nak'd hides,
Starvation and ruin, and " warching" insides :
We've proof upon proof in town, village, and shire,—
We've lots of such gobbins at Fleetwood-on-Wyre !

Lo ! while you are beggar'd, that worst of all thieves,
The tub-gutted landlord the profit receives,
Shoots up like a mushroom, and struts like a squire,
As proud as Sir Hesketh through Fleetwood-on-Wyre !

---

* A man's real name.   † A fact.   ‡ Credit.

Fat Dobson invites you to call at his trap :
Big Edmondson tempts you to call at the tap ;
And fine Mr. Hornby, with these, doth conspire,
To fleece the poor natives of Fleetwood-on-Wyre.

The " Hotel" is just let, to a Frenchman, I hear :
One Monsieur Vantiegn for some thousands a year,
Who says (but in language politer and slyer),
" I'll sheat dese sly English at Fleetwood-on-Vyre !"

Sign the teetotal pledge, and his prospects you'll mar,
And Monsieur would snuffle and mutter " Begar,"
" I can't pluck one goose, so from hence I'll retire ;
" John Bull is old sly-boots at Fleetwood-on-Vyre."

Two hundred and fifty per annum,—Tom Lunn
Has promis'd old Parker for sharing the fun ;
And, besides paying this, Tommy Lunn doth aspire
To wax independent at Fleetwood-on-Wyre.

Place your name in our book, and the mischief prevent ;
For if you refuse to pay Tommy's big rent,
Like a jackass whose bum has been pricked with a briar,
He'll soon " cut his lucky" from Fleetwood-on-Wyre.

Ah ! poor number one ! you've not used him so well,
Sink lower you could not—unless into hell ;
Teetotal would raise you a step or two higher,
Then, try it, ye drunkards of Fleetwood-on-Wyre.

Remember that time is the artisan's wealth,
And time's of no use if a man have no health ;
And sickness will vanish, and want will expire,
When sots become sober at Fleetwood-on-Wyre !

The landlord may sneer, but let those " laugh who win ;"
To-day, lads, the blest reformation begin ;
And England shall see, and, beholding, admire
The glorious example of Fleetwood-on-Wyre !

We've made a beginning, and, some of these days,
We'll set the whole town in a teetotal blaze :
The faggots *are* kindled, may God stir the fire,
And spread it like lightning through Fleetwood-on-Wyre !

THE DOINGS OF JERRY.

Tune—" The Bailiffs are coming."

The Jerry Lords tell us what good there's in drink,
But they'll be wise fellows to prove it, I think ;
These sellers are liars in praising their stuff,
And this the poor drunkards have felt long enough.
Ye drunkards, bethink you what Jerry has done,
And that will unblink you, as sure as a gun ;
For, if not too puzzling, ye slaves of the pot,
O tell us by guzzling what good you have got.
    The pleasures of drinking, O my, O my,
    You rate them, I'm thinking, too high, too high,
    For Jerry deceives you ; and give it fair play,
    It beggars and leaves you the piper to pay.

Can drink make you merry ?   It may for a night,
But in a great hurry this pleasure takes flight ;
To-day it brings laughter, makes enemies friends,
But O, the day after, what horror attends.
Still Jerry pursuing, rank madmen you prove,
But stung with the ruin of all you should love ;
The knife and the halter lay ready, you find,
But there your hands falter, for hell is behind.
    Is this to be merry, O fie, O fie,
    I tell you what, Jerry, you lie, you lie ;
    You heighten the fever with proff'ring relief,
    You barefaced deceiver, you legalised thief.

Whilst poverty scatters your last spark of pride,
And patches and tatters your skinny ribs hide;
These swipes-selling vermin, as if by design,
Have spick and span garments, oh! bless us, how fine!
And while you sit grumbling, alive, and but just,
Voraciously mumbling a butterless crust,
With your precious money those rascals command
The milk and the honey—the fat of the land.

> Your figs are but thistles, I fear, I fear;
> You pay for your whistles too dear, too dear;
> The price makes you tremble—health, money,
>   and peace—
> And just you resemble so many pluck'd geese.

A pitiful pickling your brains are, I think,
To cling to that ticking Iscariot, strong drink;
To welcome starvation, their coffers to swell,
Who death and damnation are licensed to sell.
Yes, Jerry hath made you the laugh of the town,
Beguil'd and betray'd you, and you are done brown;
Yet still to the slaughter like sheep you depart,
To buy this spoil'd water at sixpence per quart.

> From glasses and revels, O fly, O fly,
> Bid bums and blue devils good bye, good bye;
> The cap of reflection this moment put on,
> And show some affection for poor number one.

WHAT IS A SOT?

What is a sot? A heartless, perjured knave.
    Ask his poor partner whom he should have cherished.
He is a slave, to that vile lust, a slave,
    On whose fell shrine domestic love hath perished.

What is a sot? his children's deadliest curse.
    Oh! such a man the certain prey of hell is;
He spurns their guileless love, and, what is worse,
    Laughs at their clotheless backs and foodless bellies.

What is a sot ? the landlord's veriest thrall,
Who robs himself to line his fleecer's breeches,
Who gives him health and wealth, and time, and all
To drink his drugs, and hear his canting speeches.

What is a sot ? the Devil's willing tool,
Who earns enough of means to live in clover,
And yet, is never satisfied—blind fool!
Unless when reeling drunk, or half seas over.

What is a sot ? a youthful, aged man,
At thirty, worn and superannuated;
His vigour sapp'd, eyes bleared, and visage wan,—
Grey haired, affectionless, and muddle pated.

What is a sot ? that's rather hard to know:
A nondescript in habits, form, and station,
That wears the form of man, yet ranks below
The speechless, soulless, animal creation.

What is a sot ? a monstrous thing, and queer,
Which good men loathe, and worldly wise men hoot at,
Which Satan welcomes with a willing sneer,
A mark for mocking ridicule to shoot at.

What is a sot ? a self-willed wanderer, whom
The hellish hireling fastens to his tether :
A sickening mouthful for the gaping tomb,
A lump of filth and vices rolled together,

What is a sot ? a thing that walks erect,
That should for many a murder-causing bout hang ;
A dish which hungry tigers would reject,
A nasty, stinking, British ourang-outang.

What is a sot ? yon luring ale shop search,
And if you see a wretch whose skin is yellow,
Whose eyes are black, who cannot keep his perch
Upon the chair, but tumbles,—that's the fellow.

OUR OBJECT IS GRAND!

Our object is grand, don't you know what we wish ?
'Tis to make men not bottom the glass, but the dish ;
Not to guzzle strong ale, and, when swallowed, to spew,
But to buy some roast beef, and when that's done, to chew.

Our object is grand, 'tis to make men to think
Both to look what they eat, and to know what they drink :
To tell them that beggars at ale shops are made,
And that none but the landlords grow rich by that trade.

Our object is grand, 'tis to banish the glass,
Which turns a nice man into worse than an ass ;
An object of pity, a tub full of sin,
Which angels might weep at, and Beelzebub grin.

Our object is grand, 'tis to give the sot sense,
To which he at present can make no pretence ;
To put in his pocket his own hard won pelf,
Not to work for the landlord, but " fend" for himself.

Our object is grand, 'tis to give sots a hint
That landlords are wealthy from jerry's foul mint ;
And—fast as the landlord to competence jogs—
The drunkard, poor noddy, must " go to the dogs."

Our object is grand, 'tis to show the poor sot,
That while sorrow and penury darken his lot ;
The landlord just now, in the valley hard by,
Is building a house at least five stories high.

Our object is grand, 'tis to show two legg'd pigs,
That, while landlords whirl past in their coaches and gigs,
The drunkard, in weather, wet, windy, and dank,
Trots by on a " tit" that belongs to John Shank.

Our object is grand, 'tis to show ale-fill'd hacks,
That while their own wives have no clothes to their backs,
The landlady, finest in fashion's gay throng,
Like another queen Jezebel, trollops along!

Our object is grand, 'tis to show him who swills,
That while his own babes toil in steam propell'd mills,
The landlord's spoil'd young ones, with elegance dress'd,
Like ladies and lords, strut as proud as the best.

Our object is grand, you have heard what we want;
You—to save your own brass, which, at best, is but scant;
Too long you've been roll'd by that brown colour'd thief,
But now you may learn to "turn o'er a new leaf."

Our object is grand, and though landlords deride,
They know we've your weal, and good sense on our side;
Then drunkards resolve that these mountains of puff
Shall rob you no more, for they've "cabbage" enough.

Our object is grand, and we call upon all,
Who as drunkards have tasted this "wormwood and gall,"
To shun their worst foes—the decanter and cup—
And by signing our "pledge," turn the world right side up.

PINS A-PIECE.

Hie you, hie you! come with me,
And a curious sight you'll see;
Come, without one if or but,
And inspect the drunkard's hut.
Pins a-piece to look in a show,
Lots of nothing all in a row!

Look within and look without,
Look straight on and round about ;
Is it not supremely grand ?
Straw for bed and grease for sand.
    Pins a-piece to look in a show,
    Tallow for carpets all in a row!

Blown with winds, and soaked with rains,
Paper bags for window panes,
Which, when through the weather pops,
Are stopp'd up with sods and cops.
    Pins a-piece to look in a show,
    Strange contrivements all in a row !

Snails are seen upon the wall,
Up the windows spiders crawl,
A long-legged and grizzly throng,
Weaving muslin all day long.
    Pins a-piece to look in a show,
    Cobweb curtains all in a row!

There's the table,—that old door,
In the middle of the floor ;
All propp'd up with stones and bricks,
And with sundry hazel sticks.
    Pins a-piece to look in a show,
    Family fixtures all in a row !

All the pots " my Uncle " sacked,
(All but two and they are cracked),
All the tools for dinner work,
Save an ancient one-legged fork.
    Pins a-piece to look in a show,
    Tools for crutches all in a row!

There's the dish from which they feed ;
" Bums " have dished it up indeed ;
Girl and woman, boy and man,
Stick their crutches in the pan.
    Pins a-piece to look in a show,
    Two-legged grunters all in a row !

See the fender, as you stoop,
Made of an old barrel hoop;
See the kettle on the hob,
Shedding tears for Gipsy Bob.
　　　Pins a-piece to look in a show,
　　　Jobs for tinkers all in a row!

There's the chairs on which they sit,
Swallowed in a drunken fit;
All below, and all upstairs,
Bricks for stools, and stones for chairs.
　　　Pins a-piece to look in a show.
　　　Longridge* cushions all in a row!

O, what high extatic bliss,
To possess a house like this;
Cleared of all its goods by some
Landlord thief, or rascal bum.
　　　Pins a-piece to look in a show,
　　　Swill-tub scrapings all in a row!

THE DEAD WEIGHT.

Yes, England pants beneath the weight,
" The dead weight" of her greatest bane;
The ship is sinking with her freight,
And Hell usurps where Heaven should reign.

Man's direst foe—the drunkard's drink—
Spreads far and near its horrid fires;
Yet, yet professing Christians shrink
From fighting when their God requires.

Hell's deepest caverns burnt e'en now
With souls by drunkenness undone;
Before that idol millions bow,
Which damns the wretch it glares upon.

---

* A village near Preston where stone is procured,

C

While down they send their drunken hosts,
　Men, for whose souls God's Son was given ;
Sholud Jesus' captains quit their posts,
　While Hell is thus defrauding Heaven ?

We charge you, in the Saviour's name,
　Who for your sake his own life gave,
Your drunken brethren to reclaim,
　From doom more wretched than the grave.

Fight, wrestle, struggle with the foe ;
　One effort for the drunkard make !
Give this huge vice its mortal blow
　And do it now, for Jesus' sake.

HOW QUIET THE PUBLICANS ARE.

How quiet the publicans are,—not a word now
From the rascals in public or private is heard now ;
'Tis better for them that their talkers are quiet,
That they keep their loud clackers from breeding a riot.

They know that their cause is a villanous " bad un" ;
They know that the life of a sot is " a mad un" ;
This makes them quite dumb, for we've learn't 'em to
　　think, lads ;
The more they are urged, and the more they will blink,
　　lads.

The more they oppose us, the more we perplex 'em ;
The more they look big, and the more we shall vex 'em ;
Opposition justs suits us, for, sure as it grumbles,
Another big stone on the jerry-shop tumbles.

Then, let the proud villains breed strife and confusion ;
It cannot long prop this detested delusion ;
Ere long will the drunkards of Todmorden waken,
And learn, not to drink, but to save their own bacon !

AN ADDRESS TO CHRISTIAN PROFESSORS ON BEHALF OF DRUNKARDS.

Did Jesus die to pay our debt ?
  Then, such as feel the sprinkled blood,
Will, like Him, ease and self forget,
  And part with all for Zion's good.

Love bade Him quit the joys above;
  Love brought the Father's firstborn down;
And we must show our faith by love,—
  No love, no bliss ; " no cross, no crown."

For us He left a shining Heaven,
  Unbought, unbidden, undesir'd ;
And where so much is done and given,
  There must and will be much required.

Why stand ye idle all the day ?
  While drunkards—an unnumbered host—
Madly with their perdition play,
  Die without mercy, and are lost.

The true saint never thinks of self
  When battling with a damning vice ;
But gladly parts with fame and pelf,
  If God demands the sacrifice.

As Christ for him, so He, for such
  As have, by guilt, Heaven's anger braved,
Will give up all, nor deem it much,—
  Nothing, if drunkards can be saved.

Diseas'd without, diseas'd within ;
  Their case a heart of flint would melt ;
Have pity on these slaves of sin,
  Ye, who the Saviour's power have felt !

He paid your debts—extreme demands—
　　When Hell's dread prison gaped for you ;
For Christ's sake, seize your brother " brands,"
　　And snatch them from the burning too.

Oh ! while the sot to ruin drives,
　　Point out to him a different track,
And, by the magnet of your lives,
　　Attract the lust-born truants back.

Poor Zion mourns her scattered sheep,
　　And can her shepherds sleep supine ?
" The fields are white," and who shall reap ?
　　Servant of God ! the work is thine !

———

A SIMILE,

SHOWING HOW JOHN BULL'S ACHING TOOTH MAY BE CURED.

When a rotten tooth aches in an old woman's " munch hole,"
　　Sure Miss Noddy, surgeon, is sent for, who comes,
And bathes and foments with a tincture-dipped sponge, all
　　The insides and outs of her agonized gums ;
But all would not answer,—she finds she has mocked her ;
　　Her gums are still swelled, and her rotten peg shoots,
So she hurries away to a regular doctor,
　　Who cures her by plucking it up by the roots.

Such a tooth is strong drink in the head of the nation,
　　Racking Johnny with pains that are felt to his tail,
And long has that maidenly quack, " Moderation,"
　　Been trying his Nostrums, but all of them fail !
We're not a whit better,—in vain we have sought all,
　　And tried all his tinctures,—we're worse every " bout,"
And worse we shall grow, until Doctor " Teetotal"
　　Shall cure Johnny's munchers by pulling them out.

ADDRESS TO THE INHABITANTS

OF TODMORDEN.

Landlords told us from the first
 This would prove as stubble;
They must alter, ere they burst
 Our " Teetotal" bubble.
Kindled in the Heaven-taught fire,
 'Twill go out they tell us;
Disappoint their fell desires,
 Todmorden's brave fellows.

As we march, our ranks increase
 From the mere beholders;
As we march, domestic peace
 Pats us on the shoulders.
At strong drink we aim the blow,
 By his dreadful slaughters;
Help us now to lay him low
 Todmorden's fair daughters.

Evil reigns; the churches weep;
 Christ is vainly bleeding;
And, can God's own servants sleep,
 Careless, cold, unheeding?
Rather up, and meet the fray;
 War with these Philistines;
Cast the "little sup" away,
 Self-denying Christians!

Now to make sin's temples nod;
 Brethren do not dally;
For the sake of man and God,
 Round this standard rally.
Other towns for Heaven and man,
 Fearlessly combine, lads:
Foremost in the Godlike van,
 Let your valley shine, lads!

LINES

Spoken at Todmorden on the 11th February, 1848,

being the thirteenth anniversary of the teetotal birthday of

Ambrose Brook.

What, thirteen years ? And his health as good
As when he mixed " old stingo" with his blood ?
Have not his nerves grown shatter'd, trembling, weak ?
Has not the rose deserted his wan cheek ?
Does not the wind pierce through his ghost-like frame ?
Do not his friends with such a kinsman shame ?
What has he gained by his teetotal whim ?
What has the "water system" done for him ?

Ask his dear partner, and her glance implies—
"Look at our Ambrose, and believe your eyes ;
No more his appetite for jerry yearns,
He saves the pittance which his labour earns ;
Of cheerful men, he holds the foremost rank,
He owes no debt, my pocket is his bank ;
And thus we pace the downward slope of life,
A loving husband, and a happy wife."

Ask his dear children, and methinks I hear
Their blended voices ringing loud and clear—
" The bliss he caused, no mortal tongue can tell,
When first he bade the poison-shops farewell ;
And though we all have left the parent nest,
Where once we nestled peacefully and blest,
His bright example on his brood abides,
And cheers and purifies our own firesides."

Ask the old veteran, and, with joyous look,
He boldly cries—" My name is Ambrose Brook ;
Thank God ! no drunken-fit my vision dims,
Or shakes my nerves, or shackles my free-limbs ;

No liquid death pollutes my palate now,
My strongest draft is borrowed'from the cow ;
I follow mother Nature's simple plan,
A staunch teetotaller, and a blithe old man."

How deep the lesson : he who runs may read :
Men in good health no false excitement need ;
If we are men who grovel with the brutes,
" Strong drink is raging," bitter are its fruits ;
Turn a deaf ear to what your passions urge,
Yourselves and homes from vicious habits purge ;
If from this night one drunkard should abstain,
Old Ambrose Brook will not have lived in vain.

Sweet vale of Todmorden ! we claim with pride
Thy stream, and wending path, and green hill side ;
The moon's soft rays, and sun's meridian sheen,
Have rarely lighted up a livelier scene.
Oh ! if in mansion, dwelling-house, and cot,
There rose a shrine which drink invaded not,
Deck'd out by nature's hand, and free from vice,
A lovely vale would bloom like Paradise.

A RECITATION

Delivered at a Temperance Meeting, in Todmorden, by

Richard Brook, on the evening of the 11th of February,

1851, being the sixteenth anniversary of his father's

(Ambrose Brook) teetotalism.

Of winters and summers sixteen have roll'd by
Since Ambrose our system determin'd to try.—
A system whose principal doctrines are these,—
Drink milk, tea, or coffee, whichever you please.

In choosing your solids exert your best skill,
From bread to plum-pudding—whatever you will.
Retain a firm grip on the strings of your purse;
And banish " spoil'd barley,"—the Englishman's curse.

This common-sense system my father has tried,
And to make its advance is his glory and pride :
Behold him, enthron'd, like a cock on a perch,
As proud as a king, and as stiff as a church;
A sterling teetotaller, firm to the core,
As warm as a stripling, though sixty and more ;
A soldier of virtue, unstain'd with disgrace ;
The blessing of heaven on his jolly old face !

The soul of content in his countenance shines ;
There happiness writes her indellible lines;
Both able and willing to work for his bread,
The equal of any he holds up his head.
Without being rich, he is not very poor,
The awful " dun-horse " never stops at his door;
No creditor frowns, whether heavy or small,
My father can "shake a loose leg " at them all.

As husband or father, as neighbour or friend,
His children are ready his name to defend ;
How grateful they are that kind Providence spares
So long his example, his love and grey hairs;
I speak it to friends, I proclaim it to foes,
There breathes not a being more true to the cause :
Father Mathew's renown more extensive may be,
Father Brook is the model and pattern for me.

His frank smiling face makes a capital speech ;
And these are the lessons my father would teach :—
" A purse in my hand has a pleasanter look
Than my name written full in the publican's book ;
A man looks as well, as he trots o'er the flags,
In a suit of broad cloth as in tatters and rags ;
And a loaf of wheat bread, with a pound of nice chops,
Will feed a man better than barrels of slops."

The valley of Todmorden boasts not a few
Of men, like my father, to principle true ;
Who righteously war with that thief of the pot
Which ruins the shivering and penniless sot ;
Who visit his wife in her seasons of grief,
On errands of pity, and promise relief ;
The wrath of the careless and wicked outbrave,
One drunkard to rescue from guilt and the grave.

Poor slaves of intemperance ! crush'd and down trod
Beneath the foul wheels of a vile belly-god :
By signing our pledge, with a good will and strong,
You shatter the chains which have bound you so long ;
By this, and this only, is freedom ensur'd :
Thus only can life-foster'd habits be cur'd ;
Abstain for the future, past follies deplore,
And landlords shall riddle your pockets no more.

AN ADDRESS

For the Twentieth Teetotal Anniversary of Ambrose Brook,

Todmorden, February 11th, 1855.

A lovely place is Todmorden, when winter tempests lour,
Or the bright sun illumes her with vivifying power.
In shaggy rock, or whimpling brook, green wood, or smiling
    dell,
I know no spot in other climes, which her sweet nooks excel.
Her hillocks into mountains rise, as far, if not so grand,
As thine enchanting Windermere, and prouder Switzerland.

God's lavish hand hath beautified the captivating scene,
And swarming hives of labour rise the wildest glens between;
Blithe human voices strangely blend with sounds of lowing
    herds,
And childhood's laughter emulates the laughter of the birds ;
A life pervades the landscape, which, in foreign views, we
    miss :
Alas ! that sin should desecrate a paradise like this.

Yes, here man's deadliest enemy has sown his baleful tares,
And innocence on ruin's brink, stands trembling unawares;
Fell habit, with strong links of lust, like a grim tyrant, binds
The aspirations of the soul—the pinions of the mind;

AN EPISTLE

To Ambrose Brook, Lieutenant-Colonel of the 1st Regiment

of Teetotal Volunteers, Todmorden.

Good bye, old chap! not oft we've met,
But, Ambrose, you're a jolly set,
Homely and hearty, such to find
Is a hard task, among mankind.

I can't say but I rather grieve
Such comfortable folks to leave;
Not, Ambrose, that I wish to cry,
Or that I could do if I'd try.

But who does like to leave a spot
Where all his cares were half forgot?
Not many, I should think, feel so,
Nor so do I—but I must go!

Well, if I must I must, but then,
Ere long, I'll be with you again,
And then, old friend, along with thee,
We'll have a brave teetotal spree.

Oh! yes, we learn folks not to brew,
Nor drink, nor stagger,—but to chew,
Though now 'tis stiffer than a rock,
We'll give the foe another knock.

May great success our efforts crown,
May sin's great bulwarks tumble down,
May drunkenness to fly be made,
May landlord's find a better trade.

And now, good bye ! old chap stick fast.
Thanks, Ambrose, for thy favours past,
While it shall be my hope to dwell
I'll wear thee in my heart,—Farewell !

TO THE SAME.

* * * * * *

Read it old boy, to child and man,
  And, happen, they'll grow steady ;
As for thyself, thy knowledge-pan—
  Has learnt that trick already.

Go on ! for thou hast well begun,
  And though the landlords bellow,
Their rage will cause us lots of fun,—
  And fun suits thee, old fellow !

LINES ON THE DEATH OF A FRIEND,

Addressed to her Relations.

Your grief is her due, and I share in your sorrow,
  Yet we who have known her can never despond ;
Our tears as they drop on her sepulchre, borrow
  A ray of the glory that greets her beyond ;
By wishing her here we unwittingly wrong her,
  No gulf divides her from him she ador'd ;
A fetterless spirit—a captive no longer—
  A mother in Israel, sleeps with the Lord.

We lose for a season that friend so endearing,
  So lavish of kindness—unconscious of guile;
The tones of that voice, to the mourner so cheering,
  The ring of her laugh, and the gleam of her smile;
How meekly she passed through the period allotted,
  Sweet proof with rejoicing afford,
And losing a pilgrimage " pure and unspotted,"
  A mother in Israel sleeps with the Lord.

The Saviour she loved—to His servant in pity—
  Reveals the dear friend His compassion had lent,
And sorrow subsides as we muse on the city,
  To which in glad triumph she recently went;
Behind her the robe of mortality casting;
  A native of Eden—to Eden restored;
O'ershadow'd and pillow'd by love everlasting,
  A mother in Israel sleeps in the Lord.

TO JEMMY FIELDING, A P.S.

Now, 'tis high time for me to stop,
  For give me leave to let you know, sir,
That I must off to Rochdale pop,
  Your coaxing, rhyme-requesting grocer.

You're a teetotaller, 'tis true,
  That's why my tired hand yet lingers
Upon this paper, though the blue
  Cramp has laid upon my fingers.

You're welcome to these rhymes, my boy,
  Not often is my pen so yielding;
Grocer, good day, I wish thee joy
  In life or death, dear Jemmy Fielding.

WE FEAR NOT THE NUMBER NOR MIGHT

OF OUR FOES.

We fear not the number nor might of our foes,
Our hands and our hearts are engaged in this cause ;
The weal of our fatherland urges us on,
Till drunkenness cease, and the battle be won.

Oh ! now for a band of the fearless and brave
Our country to free, and our drunkards to save ;
That their households may bask, and their homes may
     wax bright
In the sunshine of peace, and the smiles of delight.

Oh ! now for a phalanx of warriors, indeed,
With truth for their swords, and good-will for their creed,
Who trust in their God, and for payment can find
A golden return, in the joy of mankind.

Our long rayless prospects begin to improve,
Our conquests have hallowed this " labour of love ;"
The dawn of a moral millennium appears,
Wake, Christians ! and shake off the slumber of years.

ADVICE TO DRUNKARDS.

Too long you poor drunkards have lavished your gains,
As wages to Jerry, for stealing your brains,
For picking your pockets, for sapping your lives,
For starving your children, for killing your wives,
For stripping you naked, like sheep that are shorn,
But "that's a long lane which has never a turn."

Let's reason together, oh ! why should your brass
Turn the landlord in fortune's rich meadow to grass ?
Why should you keep his lady,'his miss, and young spark ?
Why should you feed the bum, and his master the shark ?
Why should your goods embellish my uncle's thick shelves?
You poor, silly noddies, look after yourselves.

I know you suspect they have used you like brutes,
I guess you are sick of strong drink and its fruits,
And you have not begun to be weary too soon,
They have "peppered your bodies," they have, to some tune;
Your freedom is near, take our doctor's advice,
And you will be sav'd, without money or price.   .

Moderation pretenders would cure you by halves,
With "take it good" plasters, and "leave it good" salves;
Now, these bit-by-bit folks go the wrong way about,
The wound breeds "proud flesh," and it must be cut out,
Lest the poison should spread, and your vitals attack:
A doctor indeed !   Moderation's a quack.

I pity your case, because I've felt the rod ;
I know you may, because I do, thank God.
Heaven knows what your bodies and minds have endured,
There is a physician, and you may be cured,
No fee is required, and the worst may apply,
The remedy's sure, and God help you to try.

A TEMPERANCE SONG.

I love my ease, and ne'er denied
The comforts of a warm fire-side ;
Fair woman's beamy smiles impart
A thrill of rapture to my heart.
But are these only to be found
In the hotel's enchanted ground ?
Yes, in that happy cot serene
Where my dear wife presides as queen.

I love the burning thirst to quench
But not amid the tavern's stench ;
I'd rather take a hearty swill
Of water, from yon gurgling rill ;
Or lap the pure and snow-white juice
Which ruminating herds produce ;
While often, as I read the news,
My wife a cup of Sampson brews.

I like " good living,"—but not mine
Are costly draughts of ruby wine ;
Brown ale with folly may go down,
But I prefer roast beef done brown.
Away with porter's bitter froth,
Give me a bowl of starry broth ;
Health needs no stimulants like these,
And wine must bow to " bread and cheese."

I welcome laughter, but my laugh
Depends not on the cups I quaff ;
My mirth is gushing, guileless, wild,
As the clear chuckle of my child :
I loathe the dull, galvanic grin
Which reaches not the soul within,
Wrung from the nerves—the face to dress,
By the vile force-pump of excess.

I am no niggard,—though I strive
To keep some honey in the hive,—
A bag of gold to fall upon
Is a nice thing when age comes on :
Bright independence is a prize
Excelled by none beneath the skies ;
And in her stern and rigid school
The spendthrift is a pitied fool.

The ruling passion which pollutes
Our native land with reeling brutes,
Like other despots had his day,
But dwindles now his ancient sway.
How blest the hour when I rebelled,
From lip and home the foe expelled,
Short was the conflict, brief, but hard,
And freedom is my rich reward.

FAIR DOWN.—A TRUE TALE.

Pindaric.

A drunken man is very foolish,
Thick-headed, muddle-soul'd, and mulish;
If there be any sceptics here,
They'll think the epithets severe,
And frown.   Well, let them frown their fill,
I'll tell the truth on't, that I will.

'Twas on a sunless, rainy day,
And, as a Darwen chap would say,
            " 'Twas varra weet,"
Two drunken men came blustering and swaggering,
And belching, * * * * and hiccuping, and staggering
            Up Preston-street,
Like two acquainted, friendly pigs, they waddled on together,
Despising shame, and staring eyes, and slutch, and dirty
      weather.

      These drunken men,
Could they have seen themselves just then
      In that foul plight,
They would, themselves, have sickened at the sight;

They would have thought it wrong work,
It would have stopp'd their tongue work,
And spoil'd their maniac laughing,
And cur'd them of their quaffing,
At least, it would have done't for one short while,
They were besplashed in such a finished style:
But the drunkard cannot see himself, he's blind, completely
     blind
To bodily defects, or imperfections of the mind.

Now, hear me, what I mean,
I wish you could have seen
     Those drunken men
     Just then;
It seem'd as though the sky,
Convinc'd these sots were dry,
Resolved to slake and wash their outward skin,
While they were pouring "Tom and Jerry" in;
     For the rain fell down and soak'd them,
     And the mire sprang up and choaked them—
               Nearly.
     So they paid, I must think,
     For their crops full of drink,
     And their staggering walk,
     And their blustering talk,
They "paid for their whistles" too dearly.

You have look'd at a dog
     Which has been in the water,
With a twist, and a spring,
     What a villanous splutter
He makes when he shakes his sides.
So, if these sots had wrung their attire,
     Their drenching had been so sound,
They'd have scatter'd com-mingled rain and mire
     For many a yard around,
          So drenched were their garments and hides.

D

In this unseemly plight
They caught my sight,
As they were trudging on their reeling way
Their conversation grew quite warm,
And, as I thought, there could be not great harm
In heaiing what these "rum uns" had to say,
I followed near,
Close in their rear,
To hear if things, who really look'd like swine,
Could talk like men,—whose origin's divine.
"Jack! Jack!" bawl'd out the first,
And then he stopp'd to hiccup,
At which he stamp'd and curst,
Which forced the wretch to pickup;
And then he tried to find his tongue again,
"Jack!" he resumed, "I never yet was vain,
But tell me, as thou lovest a brimming cup,
What dost thou think of me—arn't I fare up?"

In speaking loud to make Jack hear,
He lost his balance then and there
And tumbled in the mire, and flat
He flounder'd there, like a dead bat.
Just when this sprawling sot essay'd to rise,
A smile lit up his fellow toper's eyes,
Which made the slutch-embracing fellow frown;
"Fair up!" cries Jack with a sarcastic leer,
"Fair up! old Jackey, you are out on't there,
For, dash my wig, if you are not fare down!"

This is my tale, I've nothing more to tell;
Reader, reflect upon it, fare thee well!

MODERATIONERS.

Why do the little drop men drink,
Drink where they can pike it?
What's their motive do'st thou think?
'Tis because they like it.

Why is drink so sweet to such?
Why so fond on't is he?
'Tis because the sparkling "lush"
Makes his thinkers busy.

' Tis because the "slimy posh"
Makes a wise man stupid;
That's the motive, or, e'gosh,
Cupid is not Cupid.

" Love thy neighbour as thyself,"
That's the rule of duty,
But the moderation elf
Cannot see its beauty.

Love his neighbour? Him, indeed!
Love his weaker brother?
Love thyself's his darling creed,
Care not for another.

Though the lust of drink has sent
Thousands unforgiven
To their graves,—their faces bent
Far from God and heaven.

Fraught with apathy enough,
Quite enough to freeze us,
He will calmly drink this stuff,
And he'll talk of Jesus.

Out upon him! while he drinks
(Though he does it snugly),
Selfishness in saints, methinks,
Looks confounded ugly.

Well may worldlings closely eye
Such an one's transgressions,
While his actions give the lie
To his fair professions.

Drunkenness is hell's own car
  Laden with lost millions,
And these "back door" drinkers are
  Beelzebub's postillions.

Block its way, impede its course,
  "Scotch" no wheels, but "smash them,"
On these drivers hurl your force—
  Floor, expose, and thrash 'em.

We can do without their helps,
  Can't we lads?   We'll try for't;
Shame these moderation whelps,—
  Conquer, lads! or die for't.

———

SAFETY.

Handle not, nor touch, nor taste,
Lest your ranks be in disgrace
By the careless walk of those
Who seem zealous in the cause.
Let your words and actions be
Models of propriety;
Round your passions build a fence,
Grounded upon abstinence.

Slave of custom and of lust,—
Man! thy station is the dust;
If thine eye be not too dim,
God is power—confide in him.
On that God thy burden roll,
He can save thy feeble soul;
Under mercy's pinions hide
All thy guilt, for Jesus died!

CHARGE TO THE ONSET.

The landlords alarmed at our panoply strong
  Are striving to crush us, well let 'em,
They fight in a cause which is grounded in wrong,
  And we'll beat as we've hitherto beat 'em.

Let 'em come with their paunches as bulky as tubs,
  Huge lumps of corporeal lumber,
Our abstinence fire-arms shall scatter the grubs,
  And gloriously lessen their number.

Moderation (out on it) it's out of our line,
  And shall we uphold it? No, never!
No Jerry-wag gravy for us, nor malt brine,
  But beef and spring water for ever.

These, these are our pistols fresh primed for a fray;
  Present, and make ready, and cock 'em,
And then, if these landlords assail us,—huzza!
  We'll let go the triggers and sock 'em.

TO GADSBY.

I wonder, friend Gadsby (that title should do,
For "puff," I suppose, is distasteful to you),
That a man of your calling, experience, and sense,
Should set yourself up as a "rock of offence."

If you thought, by presenting your impudent front,
To thwart us, 'twas Briton-like, reckless, and blunt,
You were wrong. When unprivileged persons intrude
On a meeting, in spite of the chairman, 'tis rude.

Our annual meeting was but for our friends,
To strengthen our cause, and further its ends,
And you know, at such times, that the voice of the chair
Should be sacred and cloth'd with omnipotence there.

You slighted that voice, and with motives as base
As would actuate friends in a similar case,
With language unfeeling, unlovely, and rash,
You spouted your frothy, irrelevant trash.

You marr'd our proceedings, and made them quite rife
With wrath and contention, and clamour and strife,
And gave him a license, whose infidel din,
Seem'd forg'd at the den of the father of sin.

Thus, sir, you dishonour'd the cause and the name
Of your peace-loving Master—the sacrificed lamb,
And, maugre our friendly entreaties and prayers,
Brought shame on your office, your name, and grey hairs.

And what was your motive? (to those who had eyes
That motive was seen in your sinister eyes),
To sneer at our pledge, and by sapping that prop,
The tide of our brilliant successes to stop.

What was the objection you pleas'd to allege
Against our distinguishing feature—the pledge?
" If you signed it, you could not conform to its rule,
Because he who trusts his own heart is a fool."

We know he's a fool, and if that be the ground
Of our members' fair hopes, 'tis unsafe and unsound;
But have we no Saviour? And is not his power
Sufficient for man in his loneliest hour?

And can't we trust him? In this life's trying scene
Man is not a passive and soulless machine,
A will-less automaton; free is his will,
To close in with grace or do what is ill.

Yes! man's a free agent, no creature of fate,
Nor doom'd to the fire of God's merciless hate;
If he has no will to obey what is writ
God loses his power to condemn or acquit.

Like you, we believe that poor mortals have strayed
From the image of God,—in which first they were made ;
Like you, to that self-crushing truth we're alive
That it's useless with inbred corruption to strive.

And does not the pledge you have scoff'd at imply
That our friends are too wise on their hearts to rely ;
And, breeder of discord, we fear not the rod
With which thou canst scourge us, our strength is in God.

TO THE LADIES.

"Woman is the weaker vessel,"
    But her sweet endearments can
Qualify the fair to wrestle
    With the stronger might of man ;
And if ever lovely woman
    Should display her welcome strength,
Arm'd with loveliness uncommon,
    That bright morning dawns at length.

* Fathers, husbands, sons, and brothers,
    Bow'd beneath the drunkard's curse,
Weeping sisters, wives, and mothers,
    Make the frightful picture worse.
Dungeons filled, asylums crowded,
    Homes despoiled, and thousands, too,
By this frightful 'sin enshrouded
    In their graves,—appeal to you.

By the hearts this vice hath riven,
    By the homes this sin hath marr'd,
By the crowds whom it hath driven
    Unreclaimed,—to their reward ;

---

* The popularity of the poem, "To the Ladies," was so great when it
first appeared, that it induced Mr. Anderton to take this and the following
verse, and incorporate it with others intended as a general appeal: Notwithstanding the other poem is given in the collection, it has been thought
proper to preserve this poem as it was first written.

By the earth, which it is thinning,
　By the hell, which ends its track,
·　Use your influence with the sinning,—
　　Lead your blinded brethren back.

Down your cheeks are grief-drops stealing
　For the drunkard's woe and pain,
By those gushes of true feeling,
　Let us not appeal in vain ;
Tears enhance your power and beauty,
　Tears will your best weapon prove ;
Women, now perform your duty !
　Speed their efforts, God of love !

————

A TEETOTALLER'S SONG.

A drunkard I was, I'm a drunkard no more,
　And the change, let me tell you, is glorious ;
No more at the ale bench I hiccup and snore,
　Nor join in their revels uproarious.
My last pot of Jerry was long ago quaff'd,
　No landlord can call me his debtor,
I have to eschew him, his shop, and his craft,
　And to like number one a bit better.

I'm out of their books, for the lawyers and " bums "
　Have long ceased to kindle my passion,
For now neither master nor " serving " man comes
　In the old six-and-eightpenny fashion,
Having no shots to pay—to my pockets nor me,—
　The arm of the law never reaches ;
Good bye to the bums ! and (I say it with glee),
　Tat-tah to the " borough-pros " leeches !

I've done with the tap-room : that dear little cot
  Is the sweetest resort of my leisure,
Whose inmates are thankful to God for their lot,
  And never lack innocent pleasure ;
Our household is truly a bundle of love,
  And, to put a top-stone to my story,
Call'd up, by his King, to a palace above,
  I've a teetotal father in glory.

This temperance can do,—it has done it for me,—
  And if, like a sceptic, thou smilest,
Or doubtest the truth of my tale, "come and see,"
  For I'm sober, who once was the vilest ;
I've my full share of health, peace, and rational bliss,
  I can weep with my friends, or be merry,
And you must confess, if our doctor does this,
  That his physic is better than Jerry.

THE TEMPERANCE HOTEL.

We've built an hotel, and, behold, it is here,
But Jowitt will sell neither strong nor small beer,
For John is teetotal, and knows very well
What's fit to be sold at a temperance hotel.

Hurrah ! for friend John, and success to the cause,
Good luck to our friends and bad luck to its foes,
Destruction to liquors invented in hell,
For that is our aim with the temperance hotel.

And when we are wed,—"if that ever will be,"
As our friends will all look for a teetotal spree,
We'll have a nice party, and cut a real swell,
At neighbour John Jowitt's—the temperance hotel.

TODMORDEN LASSES.

Before, by your sides you permit me to strut,
  Ye, whose beauties attract the beholders,
I've a word for your ear, though 'tis hard work to put
  An old head on a young pair of shoulders.

Pray, what sort of fellows have tipp'd you the wink?
  To know that is a girl's first of duties;
Are they fond of a drop—are they slaves of strong drink?
  Get to know, bonny Todmorden beauties.

Don't you know that to love, every drunkard is dead,
  And can ye, ye lovely ones, bury
Your beauties with men, whose affections are wed
  To stink, and to spue, and to Jerry?

I'll never believe it; now, therefore, my dears,
  If your lads visit Jerry-wag benches,
Oh! be masters for once, and with fleas in their ears,
  Send them home—bonny Todmorden wenches.

Honest men, modest daughters, I am sure, will conform
  To the rules of a nunnery, rather
Than marry ruffians, who cannot perform
  The duties of husband and father.

Then pester your chaps with teetotal attacks,
  And if they abandon their glasses,
Well and good, but, if not, with the bag on their backs
  Send them off—bonny Todmorden lasses.

TEETOTAL FOR EVER, SHALL WEATHER THE STORM!

Old England! though wildly thy sages have blunder'd,
While lopping the branches, forgetting the stem;
Though vainly thy priests from their altars have thunder'd,
While sharing the guilt which their sermons condemn;

Though vainly thy statesmen have rais'd our position
By suffrage extended, and sweeping reform ;
Thy sons shall be rescued from social perdition,—
Teetotal for ever, shall weather the storm !

Let Biblical sophists pervert revelation,
And force it to warrant pollution so foul,
Let sensible fools, who adore "moderation,"
Applaud a procedure which hallows the bowl ;
Let flaming professors, suspiciously pious,
Rank rebels to conscience, to custom conform :
The priest and the levites pass scornfully by us,—
Teetotal for ever, shall weather the storm !

Hurrah for the future ! The system is shaking,
Intemp'rance is shorn of its primitive strength ;
Opinion is with us, the isles are awaking
To reason, and virtue, and freedom, at length :
Old England ! rejoice in thy latter-day glory,
When vice shall not shame thee, nor folly deform ;
When preachers and people shall blazon the story,—
Teetotal for ever, has weather'd the storm !

————

A HYMN TO BE SUNG AT THE FUNERAL

OF A TEETOTALLER.

Our brother is gone ! with solemn tread
    We bear him to the gloomy spot,
The narrow house, the dreamless bed,
    Where we must shortly sleep, and rot.

So runs the sentence, " Dust to dust,"
    So earth to earth is now restor'd ;
Peace to his ashes,—and, we trust,
    His " better part " is with the Lord.

Ah! sadly would his soul have fared,
    If heaven to mark had been severe;
Or, if compassion had not spared
    This "barren tree" another year.

Long, long he slighted grace received,
    Almost too far God's power defied,
And, but for mercy, as he lived,
    This—once a drunkard—would have died.

Oh! may yon bell's deep warning sound,
    That moans our brother's last farewell,
Beget a wish in all around,
    To miss the "bitter pains of hell."

Oh! may his death some drunkard win
    From the broad way, by millions trod,
That living—he may die to sin,
    And dying, he may live with God.

THE TEETOTALLERS' ADVICE TO DRUNKARDS.

No doubt the fat publican "laughs in his sleeve,"
    And winks at his glasses well rang'd round his bar,
He crows o'er Jack Shepherd, and cries, "by your leave,
    My goose plucking system is safer by far."

Yet, though the fat bully has law at his back,
    Though government dubs him a "good man and true,"
The greasy delinquent would look rather black,
    If justice had eyes, and the devil his due!

It's stunning to think, that with eyes open wide,
    John Bull should be blind to this pitiful curse,—
And suffer the legaliz'd prig at his side
    To bleed him, and skin him, and grin in his face.

"Mine host " is a butcher, much blood he has spill'd,
  How filthy his shambles, how deadly his tools,
And when he invites you to come and be kill'd,
  You do as he bids you, like staring Tom-fools.

The villain contrives to get pursey and sleek
  On the solids he eats,—not the slops that he swills,—
While you might have fasted seven days in a week,
  Or swallow'd a shopful of Morrison's pills.

While men take their glasses, and women their drams,
  The fly from the spider will never get loose,
The wolf of the tavern will pounce on the lamb,
  The fox of the beershop will ravage the goose.

What think you ye greenhorns, and ye Johnny Raws ?
  Our system the wise, and the prudent extol ;
The simple expedient of shutting your jaws
  Would thin the dominion of grim alcohol.

Touch, taste not, nor handle one drop of their trash,
  This feasible, simple, and rational plan
Would settle in no time the publican's hash,
  And force him, as ye do, to sweat for his " scran."

How foolish the effort by method more soft,
  To break up a system upheld by the law,
You've follow'd this milk-liver'd system too oft,
  Your chains must be shiver'd, and snap't at a blow.

No matter what plans the land pirates may hatch
  To keep you in bondage, like cattle in pens,
Our pledge, like a blazing artillery match,
  Can scatter these robbers, and blow up their dens.

Why, unto yourselves the worst enemies prove ?
  Your homes and your children, your parents and wives,
Have sacred and paramount claims on your love,
  The sweat of your brows, and the toil of your lives.

Poor objects of pity, and foot-balls of wit,
    Cast hither and thither—now up and now down;
Like so many joints of roast beef on a spit,
    The landlord's have done you uncommonly brown.

The landlord, poor sot, is thy direst of foes,
    Reject then his bumpers—bright, ruddy, and clear,—
Rise gently thy thumb to the tip of thy nose,
    And bid him march off, with " a flea in his ear."

THE FELLOW WHO CUDDLES HIS TALLY.

The public house tatler, the teetotal band,
    From Bridge-mill at Whitworth are halting,
The lads in the neighbourhood stretch out their hands,
    Against their old habits revolting.
We're dish'd any moment the publican's bawl,
    'Tis ruin one instant to dally,
So Dickey must fetch out a plan for us all,
    The fellow who cuddles his tally.

The teetotal band was playing one night,
    Poor drunkards, a many were listening,
The eyes of their wives, betwixt fear and delight,
    And sweet expectation, were glistening.
When proud of his horse, of folly as proud,
    The madman cries now for a sally,
And dashes rough-shod through the peaceable crow'd,
    The fellow who cuddles his tally.

He thought he had carried the meeting by storm,
    And stared till his eyes strain'd their sockets,
As we laughed at his antics, the pitiful worm,
    And jingled the brass in our pockets.
By sticking to that we shall chase the vile crew
    From city, and hamlet, and alley,
And then, lack-a-day, what will mad Dickey say,
    The fellow who cuddles his tally.

Who kept the nice house, the old name painted out ?
  A woman it was, out upon her ;
Yet though the vile slut has no conscience about
  Her guilt, or her partner's dishonour,
She fears lest a cuckold, though tame as a louse,
  His courage and manhood may rally,
And drive, in the name of the law, from the house,
  The fellow who cuddles his tally.

That nice house outside is a hell-hole within,
  Where decency breaks from her tether,
Where manners and whoredom, and folly and sin,
  Are link'd by the devil together.
What matter's smooth words, on a subject so grave,
  Plain truth never speaks shilly shally,
That house is a nanny-shop, kept by a knave,
  The fellow who cuddles his tally.

What man will be bullied by vermin like these,
  And forc'd their potations to guzzle,
Their pockets to fill, and their whimsies to please,
  'Till penky runs out of their muzzle ?
Submit to them, no, we are thoroughly sick
  Of mixtures that gripe a chap's belly,
We'll starve out the landlords, especially Dick,
  The fellow who cuddles his tally.

---

* LINES WRITTEN IN AN ALBUM.

Madame, what can you have to do
  With such a mass of gilt-edg'd lumber ?
We've scribbling nincompoops enow,
  Nor do I wish to swell the number.

---

* Anderton did not like albums, but being urged by a lady to write something in one, he put an end to her solicitations by writing the above. The reader will see by the advice that it was written before he became a member of the Temperance Society.

An album is a precious bore,
    And, oh! it makes me melancholy
To see such rhymers wish to store,
    Your pages with ridiculous folly!

You'll think I've written *quantum suff*,—
    But, madam, burn your book this minute,
With all its wealth of mental stuff,
    Though "reverend" fools have written in it.

Can English wives find naught to do
    Save filling albums? Have a try, ma'am,
Instead of scribbling—bake and brew,
    And mend your stockings. So good bye, ma'am!

IMPROMPTU

On seeing some lines in an Album written by L. E. L., but

signed "Ellen Ward."

These lines on prayer are very well,
But they belong to L. E. L.,
And this, to be as true as brief,
Will prove that Ellen Ward's a thief.

PEEP!

A PANORAMIC VIEW OF WIG LEGISLATION.

Admission :—" Pins-a-piece."

Surely "wonders never cease,"
Valk up, gemmen, pins-a-piece!
Pins-a-piece! 'tis quite dog cheap
Such a field of fun to reap;

Pins-a-piece to peep at things
Which the "march of freedom" brings,
Pins-a-piece to look at a show,—
Modern wonders all in a row!

Freedom's tricks in '37,
Have made England just like heaven;
Public faith without a flaw!
Wages high—provisions low!
Penny cobs like shilling loaves!
Baked in Jock's "No Corn Law" stoves,
Pins-a-piece to look at a show,
Cobs where are you all in a row?

Mark the Whigs' "Dead Body Bill!"
When a pauper's pulse stands still—
"Dust to dust" is hardly read
O'er the friendless, unclaim'd dead,—
Ere the "student's" glittering knife
Maims the form yet warm with life.
Pins-a-piece to look at a show,
Whigs like butchers all in a row!

See how well these Whigs requite
Those who work for labour's right!
Dorset men sent o'er the waves
For no guilt by Whiggish knaves;
Then call'd back again—no doubt
By the "pressure from without;"
Pins-a-piece to look at a show,
Whigs turn'd tyrants all in a row!

Lo! yon Babel just arisen!
Gemmen, 'tis a "Poor-Law prison!"
Rectangle of gloom profound—
Hidden by thick walls all round;
Who are they that press thy floor?
Englishmen, because they're poor!!
Pins-a-piece to look at a show,
Whig-built dungeons all in a row!

E

In these ultra blessed times
Want and child-getting are crimes'!
" Husbands, to your partners cleave,"
Says that God whom we believe !
" Part, and no more paupers breed,"
Says Malthusian Crawfurd's creed ! !
Pins-a-piece to look at a show,
Whig-born comforts all in a row !

Paupers starve alone,—to wit—
As commissioners think fit ;
" Best to part," says Brougham Hal,—
" And," cries Little John, " they shall."
Classified must paupers dwell,
Dad, mam, lad, lass,—each a cell.
Pins-a-piece to look at a show,
Whig-made hermits all in a row !

They may meet at prayer ; but all
To the pauper's church must crawl—
There where three partitioned aisles
Baulk their recognizing smiles,
In one place, yet made like three—
Trinity in unity !
Pins-a-piece to look at a show,
Whig-plann'd temples all in a row !

They may meet at table, but
There the pauper's mouth is shut !
By the " silent system " nurst,
All are mute, though fit to burst.
What can still groan, sigh, and sob ?
" Stocks " and " nine-tails " do that job !
Pins-a-piece to look at a show,
Whig-gagg'd Britons all in a row !

Does plum pudding bless their maws ?
Does roast beef extend their jaws ?
Beef and pudding !   Nay, nay, nay !
That's the hell-born Tory way !
That would yield no treasury grist,
Says our Scotch " economist."
Pins-a-piece to look at a show,
Whig State-tactics all in a row !

Hear the Board its will pronounce—
Weigh their diet ounce by ounce!
We must save—then so contrive,
Just to save their souls alive !
Let them have the coarsest stuff,—
Fifteen-pence a week's enough!
Pins-a-piece to look at a show,
Whig-spread banquets all in a row !

Whigs don't kill their slaves at once
By a blow upon the sconce !
But they starve with right good will,
Piecemeal, bit by bit they kill ;
Thankful when we go to pot,
In the Paupers' Hall to rot.
Pins-a-piece to look at a show,
Whig-like murderers all in a row !

Thus Whigs stop the pauper's breath,
Save, by " clamming" men to death !
Scrape from British blood and bones
Brass to pay their " salaried drones."
What do these sage Britons ? zounds !
Nothing ! save the pension pounds !
Pins-a-piece to look at a show,
Whig " retrenchments " all in a row !

*　　*　　*　　*　　*　　*　　*

Is this merry England? Yes:
She who was earth's queen? It is.
" Look on this—and look on that !"—
While I just un-poke the cat !
'Tis the work of thimble-rigs!"
Jock says " rally round these Whigs !"
Pins-a-piece to look at a show,
Jocks and Melbournes all in a row !

Heed not Crawfurd's "liberal prate"
He's a leach—I calculate—
And he'll follow—in thy track—
Otty's filly ! Stamp-house Jack !
Place he'll buy—and as to price
Sawneys are not over-nice !
Pins-a-piece to look at a show,
Jocks and Lollies all in a row !

Some say I'm a turn-coat, oh !
Poor old Cobbett curst this law,
So did honest British Hunt,
So does Oastler plain and blunt,
Parker's curse has found a vent,
But Jock's " silence gives consent."
Pins-a-piece to look at a show.
Jocks and Russells all in a row !

Valk up gemmen ! Gaze your fill !
You who loathe this cursed bill
Bury all your party gall,
" Extremes meet," for sake of all,
Join to throw this Scotch bug out.
And, your showman, I will shout,
Pins-a-piece to look at a show.
Nothing uttering, " Cheese-cake " Joe !
Crawfurd muttering, " It's nae go !"
Segar sputtering, " Curse the foe !"
Barker stuttering, " Dit-dit-to !"
Four tamed "mad dogs " all in a row !

TO MR. W. HARRIS.

A few days since, dear Harris, it was my lot
To read your second letter in the *Pilot,*
From which I learned how fancy had deceiv'd you,
And how some late occurrences had griev'd you ;
For, notwithstanding your long canvass list,
The president's a non-phrenologist,
And writhing with this sore and sad defeat,
Your body still must take a common seat ;
Nor wonder then, tho' hearts at ease may smile
At your epistle, and its acid style ;
No marvel, with your mind in such a state,
If what you scribble smacks of Billingsgate ;
For shame breeds strife, and, therefore, words severe
Are what, from you, we may expect to hear,—
For ah ! " a wounded spirit who can bear ?"

'Twere bitter mockery to console thee now,
When " Ichabod " is written on thy brow,
Thy glory is departed, thou ar't cross'd
In thy ambition, and thy labour's lost ;
Thy long and deep acquaintance with the science
On which was plac'd thy strongest, sole reliance,
Thy friends have suffered this prime prop to fall,—
Oh ! " this was the unkindest cut of all."
Does not the ancient British proverb say,
That " where there is a will there is a way ?"
'Tis false ! for most determined was thy will
The chair of the phrenologists to fill :
Alas ! thou art a private member still.

Yet surely, doctor, 'tis of no great use
To seek by lies, your rival to traduce,
Or bring him from his perch to this low level,—
For falsehood is the weapon of the devil ;
Yet thy whole letter with the truth at war is.
Did some she-demon whelp thee, Doctor Harris ?
Are not thy statements of the Council's acts
At shameless, barefac'd loggerhead with facts ?

Why soil good paper, and why waste good ink ?
A world, so " wide awake," as soon could think
That hell is quite as fair a place as heaven,
As that six any things are more than seven.
By common numeration thou art " done,"
For all arithmetics through which I've gone
Make seven, nor more nor less than 6 + 1 :
And by that one thy foeman was elected,
And by that one poor Harris was rejected,
For that one's sake let " figures " be respected.
Still, you will not this humbling truth confess ;
You strive to prove the greater is the less,—
Oh ! what more glaring could your foes require
To dub you blockhead, and to brand you liar ?

In pity to your cranium's confirmation,
Accept, dear sir, my deep commiseration,
You are a fool in deed, as well as name,
And this your skull's developments proclaim :—
Your frontal regions are depress'd, sir, but
The right and left sides of your occiput
Are grac'd with organs of tremendous size,
Just where the love of approbation " lies !"
And nearer to the centre, sir, you seem
To own above your share of " self-esteem,"
And lower down, no hat, however wide
Could your huge lumps of " combativeness " hide,
And on the top sits " firmness " thron'd in state,—
The *crowning* wonder of your wondrous pate.

Hence, sir, your previous canvass, zeal, and fuss,
And whence they sprang were manifest to us ;
And your mad movements, " after the division,"
We could have prophesied with nice precision.
Impell'd by self-esteem, your thoughts ran thus :—
" The chair is vacant, and thou art the man ;"
" Rise," mutter'd Love of Approbation, " rise,
None is so fit, and, if I may advise,
Make no delay, and never rest content
'Till thou art William Harris, president !

In the requir'd attainments you excel,
And spectàcles become a chairman well."
"Yes," you replied, "the post is mine, I'll win it,
And fill it like a gentleman—when in it!"

The great day came,—the fav'rites were propos'd,—
The members voted,—the election clos'd ;—
Oh! that which follows, in my gizzard sticks,—
Lomas had seven, and Harris only six!

Smarting, as you then did, at this defeat,
Pierc'd in your love of praise and self-conceit,
Up to your aid your "combativeness" starts,
And at the victor, like a bull dog, darts.
"Again," you cried, "I do and will insist
That none preside, but a phrenologist ;
And for that honour I will struggle yet,
In spite of Corless, and his chuckling pet."
So your first letter, hot with it's own fervour,
Hiss'd in the *Pilot*, blaz'd in the *Observer*,
In sooth, it was a matchless "paper bullet,"
Though ill-adapted for the public gullet,
Yet pass'd it not unheeded, for thy folly
Was answer'd by a well-directed volley,
Which did thy patience utterly confound,
And gave thy vanity—a mortal wound.

Then stiff-neck'd "firmness" stood thy friend, and when
This organ influences a mortal's pen
It renders him unwilling to draw back, as
An Irish hog, or stiffer English Jack-ass ;
And, prompted by thy firmness, grown self-willy,
Thy vengeance forg'd another sword, my Billy,
But in its *Pilot*-sheath the weapon tarries
Pointless and rusty as thy wit, dear Harris.

Lo! no man heeds thy worse than monkey tricks,
And though thou kickest—'tis against the pricks ;

This ceaseless, three-weeks' ransack of the brains,
These waking tremors, and these dreaming pains,
This constant racking of thy ruling bumps,
Have gain'd thee nothing but contempt and thumps ;
The public voice thy selfish sphere derides,
Upon the private form thy * * * abides,
And worst of all, the cause of thy despair,
The pet of Corless, fills the presidential chair.

A NEW SONG.

Tune :—" The girl I left behind me."

" To Sir Robert Peel, the poor of England are indebted for the boon
of untaxed bread."—COMMON SAYING.

Duke Richmond mock'd a nation's woe,
   And hugg'd his Corn-law hobby ;
And what could Cobden, Bright, and Co.
   Have done without Sir Bobby ?
The " League " subscribed a good round sum,
   And printed tons of paper ;
While farmers dubb'd it—" All a hum,"
   And our petitions—"Vapour !"

Loud was the noise without the " House,"
   But stagnant the interior ;
There needed one the state to rouse,
   To party-ties superior :
The efforts of the " League " were great,
   But paralyzed in action ;
There lack'd a chieftain, good and great,
   To burst the bonds of faction.

Though Duncan's penny gun was cock'd,
  And fired amongst the number,
Monopoly had firmly lock'd
  The Mersey, Clyde, and Humber;
Protection grinn'd when Liberals fumed,
  And Villiers launched his "measure;"
To empty bellies we were doom'd,
  For bread was at high pressure.

Sir Robert left the "House" no choice,
  He captured young and hoary;
And link'd, by his bewitching voice,
  Whig, Radical, and Tory;
And with this weapon multiform,
  By dint of sheer persuasion,
The hero quell'd the rumbling storm,
  Which shook the startled nation.

He welded brains of adverse sorts,
  And solder'd all their quarrels;
Till by their aid—corn fill'd our ports,
  In French and Yankee barrels;
And while this gallant game he play'd,
  State quack and swindler rumpling,
He opened Britain's doors of trade,
  And doubled Britain's dumpling.

Her statesman's death—the realm laments,
  The poor his praise are singing;
While unto him brave monuments
  Are everywhere upspringing;
Wide Europe ratifies his fame,
  The man of huge endeavour;
And coming times shall bless the name,
  And honour Peel for ever!

Shall Bury then reject his son,
  And prove herself ungrateful ?
His native town shall never don,
  A character so hateful;
Sir Bobby changed our dismal notes,
  To ditties brisk and merry;
And by our grateful, hearty votes,
  His son shall go for Bury !

IO TRIUMPHE ! OR, LORD DUNCAN'S FINALE.

Air :—" Sound the Loud Timbrel."

Scratch the Scotch fiddle, from Stand to Pigslee,
The boasters are worsted, and Bury is free !
  Barebones, parading his true Brunswick breed up,
    To vote for Lord Sawney, was thrash'd for his pains ;
  And vainly was Freetown commissioned to lead up
    Her riff-raff batallions—all sheawt and no brains !
Scratch the Scotch fiddle, from Stand to Pigslee,
Lord Duncan has vanished,—and Peel is M.P. !

Swell the shrill bag-pipes, from Stand to Pigslee,
The humbugs are routed, and Bury is free !
  Pack-poising pedlars—Scotch, clannish, and feudal,
    Would vote for a devil in " tartan and kilts;"
  But thin was their phalanx, for Duncan Mac-Noodle
    Has dropp'd with a whack from his ginger-bread stilts !
Swell the shrill bag-pipes, from Stand to Pigslee,
Lord Duncan has mizzled,—and Peel is M.P. !

Twang the big banjo, from Stand to Pigslee,
The Quacks are well physick'd, and Bury is free !
  Tied in " the sack," snd impaled on fame's stretcher,
    Young Camperdown struggles, grimaces, and grins,
  With the spikes of the war-club of brave Dr. Fletcher,
    Tattooing his carcase, like Brummagem pins !
Twang the big banjo, from Stand to Pigslee,
Lord Duncan has bolted,—and Peel is M.P. !

SWIG AWAY!!

A nobleman witty,
Post hast for Bath city,
In language not pretty,
And tones very gritty,
Pours forth this wild ditty,
And wops his committee.

Tune :—" Nix My Dolly, Pals, Fake Away."

My committee came out as Simon Pure,
       Simon Pure,
How they chew these tickets for drink, for sure,—
       Swig away.
But I, their gaffer, am not so nice,
I must walk to the senate,—whate'er the price,—
     Draw the spigots and swig away.

This jaw about " morals " is all my eye,
And he who scribbles it—writes a lie ;
       Swig away.
To act on a mob with a telling force,
You must fuddle the noddle, and line the purse,—
     Draw the spigots and swig away.

So chatter away, my virtuous scribe,
If Peel gives tipple, my pals must bribe,—
       Swig away.
The hammers to clench outstanding votes
Are yellow queen's heads, and five pound notes,—
     Draw the spigots and swig away.

In the city of Bath we'd glorious fun,
When rhino and penkey the battle won,—
       Swig away.
And the " Mosses " shall honour the foaming brim,
For in lashings of lush my geese shall swim,—
     Draw the spigots and swig away.

THE POOR, GOD BLESS 'EM!

Let sycophants bend their base knees in the court,
   And servilely cringe round the gate,—
And barter their honour, to earn the support   .
   Of the wealthy, the titled, the great;
Their guilt-piled possessions I loathe, while I scorn
   The knaves—the vile knaves—who possess 'em,
I love not to pamper oppression, but mourn
   For the poor, the robb'd poor,—God bless 'em!

Let tyranny glitter in purple and gold,
   The sheen and the costly array;
Let idiots take pleasure in what they behold
   'Till the puppet shows vanish away;
I turn from such pageants as these, for I know
   Whose gold bought the gew-gaws which dress 'em;
I turn from such splendour to brood o'er the woe
   Of the poor, the starved poor,—God bless 'em!

Let legalis'd wrong domineer over right,
   And want be accounted a crime;
Let barefaced dishonour put virtue to flight,
   And traitors exult in their prime;
Let the pride-trampled mob feel the venomous claws
   Of the vultures who strip and oppress 'em;
I care not: my soul is alive in the cause
   Of the poor, the stung poor,—God bless 'em!

Let the halls of our foemen, like Solomon's, shine
   With jewels, and echo with mirth;
While cellars, and dungeons, and garrets confine
   The bravest and best of the earth;
I'll not be that slave of these upstarts, who soils
   The knee which he bends to caress 'em;
Give me the unbought gratulations and smiles
   Of the poor, the warm poor,—God bless 'em!

And what, though discretion would check me, and say,
"The wrath of your foes will be roused?"
I'll fight against self if it stand in the way
Of the cause which my heart has espoused;
The poor are my brethren, and for them I part
With honour and those who possess 'em,
For, oh! while a pulse bespeaks life in my heart
It will throb for the poor,—God bless 'em!

A WATER DRINKER'S RHAPSODY.

See! our glasses are not fill'd
With fermented nor distill'd,—
'Tis a liquid fool's refuse,
That which Jah-Jehovah brews.
What with water can compare?
Pure as ether, free as air,
Bright as drop in pity's eye,
Sweet as breath of Araby.

Here's a bumper! drink it up,
Life is lodg'd within the cup,
Quaffing this, you waste no wealth,
Brace your nerves, and guard your health.
Boon most common, yet the best,
Harmless as a mother's breast;
Ever welcom'd with delight
By the sterling Rechabite.

Tempt no more, 'tis labour vain,
Sherry pale or red champagne,—
Give me water, Hermon's dew,
Clear as yon wide arch of blue.
Nature's recipe for thirst,—
Ne'er did man, by art accurst,
Remedy for that invent,
Like our virgin element.

Stimulants exhaust the frame,
Drunkard's play a losing game,—
Purchase, by their beastly whims,
Aching heads and shaking limbs :
But the draught that, in the wild,
Cheer'd poor Hagar's fainting child,—
And life, strength, and freedom brings,
Like the source from whence it springs.

Laughing in the mazy rills,
Leaping down the giant hills,
Sleeping in the glassy lakes,
Where no breeze a ripple makes ;
Or in teeming showers of love,
" Dropping fatness " from above,
On the scorch'd and arid sod,
Best of all the gifts of God.

Fount ! whose droppings did suffice
Sinless man in Paradise,
Blessed cup which once did quell
Jesu's pangs at " Jacob's well."
Type of what his grace imparts
To believing, broken hearts ;
Well of life, whose running o'er,
Those who drink shall thirst no more.

RAILWAYS AND OTHER WAYS.

Some fifty years sincé and a coach had no power
To move faster forward than six miles an hour,
Till Sawney Mc.Adam made highways as good
As paving stones crushed into little bits could,
Then Coachee, quite proud of his horseflesh and trip,
Cries, " Go it, ye cripples," and gave them the whip,
And ten miles an hour, with the help of the thong,
They put forth their mettle, and scampered along.

The present has taken great strides of the past,
For carriages run without horses at last ;
And what is more strange,—yet it's truth, I avow,—
Hack-horses themselves are turned passengers now ;
These coaches alive go in sixes and twelves ;
And, once set in motion, they travel themselves,
They'll run thirty miles while I'm cracking this joke,
And need no provisions but " pump milk" and coke ;
With their long chimneys they skim o'er the rails
With two thousand hundredweight tied to their tails.
While Jarvey in stupid astonishment stands,
Upturning both eyes and uplifting both hands,
" My nags," he exclaims, betwixt laughing and crying,
Are good 'uns to go, but you devils are flying.

NATURE.

" How beautiful is all this visible world."—BYRON.

There's something bright and glorious
    In the sun's first earthward glance,
When from his bed he riseth
    Like a giant from a trance,
Or when the eye o'erpowering
    With his full meridian ray,
O'er heaven's cerulean pavement
    He hurries on his way.

There's something vast and glorious
    In the sea, the deep profound,
Who claspeth, like a lover,
    The earth, his mistress, round ;
As an infant's sleep unruffled,
    Or tossing the glittering brine,
Dark, dread, and pathless ocean,
    What majesty is thine !

There's something fair and glorious
  In this little speck of ours,
In the plumes of her winged warblers,
  And the painting of her flowers,
In her fresh and vernal carpet,
  In her pebbled, troubled rills,
In her wild untrodden forests,
  And her everlasting hills.

There's something far more glorious,
  In the faith that says "I know,
From the void and formless chaos,
  Who bade these wonders grow!"
Bend, reverently, my spirit,
  Before that being fall,   `
Whose wisdom first created,
  Whose power sustaineth all.

FLEETWOOD-ON-WYRE.

"The age of miracles is past."—COMMON SAYING.

So says some old grey beard, who turns up his nose,
And shutteth his spectacled eyes as he goes,
Who, when he first heard of a steam-engine, sighed
At man's growing folly, or laughed till he cried,
Who stuck to his text, though he stared aghast,
When, swift as a comet, a train hurried past,
And in his sage pate drew this inference, pat,
I'm sartain Ow'd Nick has a finger in that.

"Have miracles ceased?" Are the workers all dead?
Before ye affirm it, just think where ye tread,—
Five brief years ago, and on this very spot
All nature ran wild, and improvement was not;
The chill wastes of Lapland could only compare
With wild "Rossall Warren," unsheltered and bare,
And here, where the sole of man's foot found no rest,
The rabbit had house-room, the sea gull a nest.

But see, what have talent and enterprise done?
A beautiful town from the wilderness won,
The streets with the proudest in Britain may vie,
The spire of the temple salutes the blue sky,
Her baths so unrivalled, enough to impart
Ineffable joy to a Mussulman's heart,
And, wonder of wonders, the glorious hotel,
Where Royal Victoria (God bless her!) might dwell.

How vainly our neighbours her overthrow seek,
Up-crying the Ribble,—that pitiful creek—
(If offered as wages, their clerk would refuse,
The yearly amount of their " Custom House dues "),
As vainly the anger of ocean is sped,
Against the town's bulwark—her noble pier-head;
Her harbour is studded with funnels and sails,
And snug in her berth is the huge " Prince of Wales."

Ye dwellers in towns, to whom seldom is given
To breathe, as God gives it, the free air of heaven;
Haste, haste! to our newly formed paradise flee,
And quaff it in puffs, as it blows from the sea,—
The railway invites, and, if marvels you crave,
Your track lies thro' valley, o'er mountain, and wave,
Go on, and, redeemed from the sea-weed and mire,
Behold that true miracle, Fleetwood-on-Wyre.

TEETOTALISM IN HARWOOD LEE.

Too long our drunken neighbours
    Have shamed the mindless brute,
But Heaven has crown'd our labours
    With a rich crop of fruit.
The vice, which long did cover
    Our land, begins to flee,
And now we can discover
    A change in Harwood Lee.

F

Drink made our place a poor hole,
  Its natives ragg'd and wan,
But when we brought our " Cure all"
  They came and tried our plan !
They found it milk and honey;
  No badge shop slaves are we ;
They trade with ready money,
  The lads of Harwood Lee.

Our neighbours' wives were beaten,
  Their best affections chill'd,
Their flesh by hunger eaten,
  Their eyes by sorrow fill'd ;
But now in town nor city
  No happier dames we see ;
They're clean and neat and pretty,
  The wives of Harwood Lee.

The drunkard's little darlings,
  So sunk in look and deed,
Provok'd the bitter snarlings
  Of Jerry's upstart breed ;
But now they look as stately,
  As poor man's child should be,
And trudge to school quite gaily,
  The lambs of Harwood Lee.

The drunkard's house was empty,
  No bacon on the hooks,
But now there's peace and plenty,
  And, oh, how nice it looks ;
No quarrels, so unsightly,
  Disturb domestic glee,
But love illumines brightly
  The homes of Harwood Lee.

And, best of all, our lasses
  The drinking trade condemn ;
And lads who like their glasses
  Will have small chance with them.

Temperance must blow love's bellows,
   Or they will ne'er agree ;
They'll not have drunken fellows,
   The girls of Harwood Lee.

Great things are done already,
   And God our cause does own ;
Be ready and fight steady
   Till Jerry be o'erthrown ;
Mind not the toil or danger,
   And victors you shall be,
And drunkenness a stranger,
   Not known in Harwood Lee.

SONG

Sung at Todmorden on the 11th February, 1846.

Tune—" The day we went a gipsying."

What means this exultation,
   That glitters in our eyes ?
It is because the sparkling bait
   We laugh at and despise ;
Yet once we were poor sensual slaves—
   Few even such so low—
In the days we went a revelling,
   A long time ago.

Our household gods are happy,
   Our wives and children dear,
And peace and love and rapture now
   Their mounting spirits cheer ;
Yet want had lengthened every face,
   And every heart was woe,
In the days we lived as revellers,
   A long time ago.

As those who live by labour,
    (No better we desire),
Our homes are snug as homes can be,
    And decent our attire ;
Like Falstaff's ragged regiment,
    We cut another show,
In the days we went a revelling,
    A long time ago.

Now God be thanked for freedom,
    From raging appetite,
Described by one of wise renown,
    As worse than serpent's bite ;
A close shut mouth, a manly will,
    Disarmed our subtle foe,
On the day we left off revelling,
    A long time ago.

A fig for moderation,
    That web by Satan spun,
Which tempts the half-recovered slave,
    To be again undone ;
In abstinence our safety lies,
    As our whole lives will show,
Since the days we left off revelling,
    A long time ago.

SONG.

Tune—" My Girl, my Friend, and Pitcher."

Ye who are fond of worldly wealth,
    Go take your fill in hoarding treasure ;
Ye sots, go wallow still in filth,
    And guzzle rum, and call it pleasure ;
Go, take your fill of such like bliss,
    But, howsoever sweet you find them,
Ye simpletons beware of this—
    They always leave a sting behind them.

TEETOTALISM TRIUMPHANT.

Tune—*" Old England for ever shall weather the storm."*

Old England! though madly thy sages have blunder'd,
  When lopping the branch and forgetting the stem :
Though wildly thy priests from their altars have thunder'd,
  While sharing the guilt which their sermons condemn :
Though vainly thy statesmen have raised our position
  By " Suffrage extended" and sweeping " Reform,"
Thy sons shall be rescued from social perdition,—
Teetotal for ever shall weather the storm.

Let biblical sophists pervert revelation,
  And force it to warrant pollution so foul;
Let sensible fools who adore " moderation,"
  Applaud a procedure which hallows the bowl!
Let flaming professors, suspiciously pious,
  Rank rebels to conscience—to custom conform :
The priest and the Levite pass scornfully by us,—
Teetotal for ever shall weather the storm!

Hurrah for the future!—The system is shaking,
  Intemp'rance is shorn of its primitive strength ;
Opinion is with us—the isles are awaking
  To reason, and virtue, and freedom, at length.
Old England! rejoice in thy latter-day glory,
  When vice shall not stain thee, nor folly deform,—
When preachers and people shall blazon the story—
Teetotal for ever *has* weathered the storm !

———

THE CHRISTIAN POET.

" The heavens declare the glory of God, and the firmament
sheweth his handywork."—The Psalms.

Sweet chords in sound abhorrent
  His listening fancy hears
In the roaring of the torrent,
  In the clashing of the spheres,

In the elemental battle,
　In the hoarsest wind that raves,
In the thunder's loudest rattle,
　And the din of tossing waves.

Far, far as fancy wanders,
　Bright shapes the earth assumes,
Where the rippling stream meanders,
　And the mountain daisy blooms,
In the liquid drop that staineth
　The violet's purple dye,
And the richer gem which raineth
　From woman's sparkling eye.

On, on! as fancy dashes
　Fresh glories strike the sight,
In the blue electric flashes,
　And the glow-worm's silvery light,
In the thickly studded alley,
　In the wrack through ether driven,
In the soft reposing valley,
　And the blazing pomp of heaven.

Religion from creation,
　Like honey, he distils,
And sacred contemplation
　The raptured gazer fills,
As step by step ascending
　He spurns the earth's green sod,
And flesh and spirit bending,
　He blesses Nature's God.

LINES ON THE DEATH OF A YOUNG LADY,

Addressed to her Family and Friends.

"There is a time for all things," joy and sadness
　Will, in their turn, the eye and memory steep,
And though philosophy may count it madness,
　When friends depart, 'tis nature's "time to weep."

Nor are we bidden by our God to smother
 Tears for kind hearts to death's embraces crept,
For David mourned for Jonathan, "his brother,"
 And at the grave of Lazarus "Jesus wept."

Sweet is the sob that bruised affection beareth,
 And oft I muse how bitter death would be,
If, when my soul his tabernacle leaveth,
 No brimful eye could spare a drop for me.

No wonder, then, that sorrow's briny traces
 Have in your cheeks worn many a channeled spot,
For from the circle of familiar faces,
 One hath departed and returneth not.

No marvel, if your quivering lips should falter,
 And sounds of wail mix with the voice of prayer,
When, kneeling round the dear domestic altar,
 Your lifted eyes behold no Hannah there.

Weep on, weep on! yet mingle faith with sorrow,
 And Hope's sweet balm will mitigate the sore,
For death is but the prelude of a morrow,
 When souls shall re-unite and part no more.

Paint not your loss to me, I know the story,
 Why Hannah here to Hannah there prefer?
Though she may never leave her rest in glory,
 Through the strait gate you may go home to her.

Why look on earth for lasting habitations?
 This place is not your rest, awake! arise!
Haste to the city which has no foundation,
 "Not made with hands, eternal in the skies."

Then seek the cure for hearts with grief oppress'd,
 Then find your dead alive, your lost restored;
There dwell the ransomed, glorified, and bless'd,
 And there she is, for ever with the Lord.

TO ELIZABETH MILLS, ROCHDALE,

On receiving a letter from her bridesmaid, impressed with the motto " Dinna forget."

Sure fancy is dull, or I'm not so clear headed
   With words at command, as in days passed away :
I promised some rhymes when Eliza was wedded,
   And married thou art, but the rhymes, where are they ?
And Jane, the dear bridesmaid—exacting as beauty,—
   Demands the unflinching discharge of the debt,
And seals the dispatch, which recalls me to duty,
   With love's sweet remembrancer—" dinna forget."

From the arms of thy mother, at length thou has ventured,
   To a coveted home with the man of thy choice ;
In him all thy hopes and affections are centred,
   And in that decision I greatly rejoice.
Remember thy vows, and adhere to the letter,
   Nor give thy affianced one cause to regret—
Constrain him to bear the conjugal fetter—
   I urge this upon thee—and " dinna forget."

I pray that thy lot may be speckless and cheerful,
   As friend the most sanguine can ask for a friend ;
In regions like this—where the gay and the tearful—
   The storm and the sunshine—so frequently blend,—
The married have power to repress and to smother
   The cares that annoy, and the sorrows that fret,
And earth will be heaven if ye love one another—
   Then act on the precept—and " dinna forget."

Now ties may await thee, a mother's sweet title
   Perchance may be thine, though procured with its smart;
But the lisp of thy child will be ample requital
   For bodily pangs and misgivings of heart ;
What draughts of pure rapture a woman is quaffing,
   When first she embraces her first little pet ;
As prone on her lap he lies crowing and laughing—
   Then haste to possess one—and " dinna forget."

Alas ! we exist in a scene of mutation,
Where causes, most trifling, our love can estrange ;
Yet faith knows an Eden of bright consummation,
Where life is perennial, and hearts never change ;
Earth's buds of affection, so fragrant and vernal,
The blight of unkindness may wither them yet ;
Yet heaven may be thine, and its joys are eternal,—
Oh strive for admission—and " dinna forget."

TO A FRIEND,

Who trembled at the thought of Dying.

True, Christian, true, we all are dying mortals,
The sentence passed on all of woman born,
Will force us through the grave's terrific portals,
For " dust thou art, and shalt to dust return."

Alas ! and must we leave the scenes we cherish,
Our homes, and friends affectionate and fond,
And in the tomb sleep like the beasts that perish,
Without one glimpse of happiness beyond ?

Nay, Christian, nay, not thus we read the promise,
" The woman's seed shall bruise the serpent's head,"
Here is a hope which death can ne'er take from us,
The Saviour liveth, he liveth who was dead.

He liveth, who was dead, let this reflection
Wipe any tear from sorrow's glistening eye,
He conquered death, and by his resurrection,
" He that believes in him shall never die."

Death, friendly death, unlocks a bright hereafter,
And seen by faith, his sharp relentless knife,
Despite the worldling's sneers, the atheist's laughter,
Clears the soul's passage to eternal life.

Lo ! Christ is risen beyond the grave's dominions,
  And through the power of his victorious love,
We his joint heirs, upborne on Hope's strong pinions,
  Shall mount to Eden, our " sweet home " above.

Poor trembling saint, let not thine heart be troubled,
  Nor with the dread of death the mind oppressed,
But be thy faith and love and patience doubled,
  For time is short, and this is not our rest.

Read and believe redemption's wondrous story,
  To him who fights and conquers shall be given,
For conflict here, the victor's crown of glory,
  For death's cold box a blood-bought throne in heaven.

TO A YOUNG LADY FROM INDIA,

Who was deprived of both parents there, previous to her

departure for England.

Oh! welcome, lonely stranger,
  To the island of the free,
For where thy earliest years were pass'd,
  Thy home shall never be ;
The deep sea rolls between thee
  And that unforgotten shore,
Which thou, with lisping Indian girls,
  Wert 'customed to explore.

Yes, thou hast looked thy latest
  On that ever cloudless sky,
And thou hast sought thy father's home
  To breathe a while, and die.
But, ha ! how barren and how cold,
  Compared with that bright land,
When far as mortal ken can pierce,
  Her sunny vales expand.

Yet, thou art not alone, sweet girl,
  Thy orphan sister, dear,
In thy rejoicing will rejoice,
  And give thee tear for tear,
Her strong affection rivals thine,
  And will not let thee prove
The nameless grief of those who love
  When "none are left to love."

What tho' our clime be changeful,
  And our mountains bleak and bare ;
What tho' our skies with India skies
  We never may compare ;
What though our feeble sun doth scarce
  Dissever night from day,
Our hearts are warm, and, if they can,
  Shall chase thy tears away.

Then welcome, lonely stranger,
  To the island of the free,
For, where thy earliest years were passed,
  Thy home shall never be :
The deep sea rolls between thee
  And that unforgotten shore,
Whose blooming bowers shall glad thy eyes,
  And fill thy heart no more.

LINES

On the death of Two Factory Children, to be Worked in

a Sampler by their Little Sister.

Farewell ! my brother Thomas ;
  Yet, wherefore should I weep,
Though he be taken from us,
  In death's cold arms to sleep ?
From tears and pain to save him,
  From bonds of sin and clay,

The Lord, the Lord who gave him,
  Hath taken him away.
By God's free grace forgiven,
  His servitude is o'er,
Our Thomas is in heaven,
  And lives for evermore.

Good bye ! my little sister ;
  Ah ! little did I fear
How soon, when last I kissed her,
  She'd leave me lonely here ;
Yet glad that death o'ertook her,
  For she's alive and well,
Free from the " overlooker,"
  And harsher " factory bell,"
The grave her bondage closes,
  Poor Mary Ann's at rest,
The weary lamb reposes
  Upon the shepherd's breast.

Dear Saviour, meek and lowly,
  Affliction makes me bold,
I'm vile, but thou art holy,
  Oh, take me to thy fold,
My playmates have departed
  To better worlds above,
And I am broken hearted,
  And pining for their love,
Kind God of the oppressed,
  Whose death has set us free,
Oh, in that hour so blessed,
  Let there be room for me.

THE SABBATH.

How barren, how cheerless, how hopeless our lot,
  And earth what a prison unblessed,
If he, " who is rich in compassion," had not
  Appointed these portions of rest ;

Loved seasons, exempt from the toils and the cares
 With which our journey is rife,
Sweet flowers springing up in a wild field of tares,
 Green spots in the desert of life. .

O ! loud let our praises ascend unto God
 That one day is granted in seven,
On which—while forgetting the perishing clod—
 Our soul may hold converse with heaven ;
Dear moments of peace and external repose,
 When man talks with God as a friend,
Bright types of a service which never shall close,
 A Sabbath which never shall end.

We claim of the Lord what his conflict hath won,
 That ultimate fruit of his love,
The rest which remains for his people alone,
 A Sabbath eternal above ;
O that we may reach that blessed shore,
 The seat of the glorious J. A. M.,
And join the "great multitude" who sing evermore,
 "Salvation to God and the Lamb."

THE "NILE" (STEAMER).

What craft is that in Morecambe Bay,
 So faultless in her rig,
Which onward speeds her placid way,
 As lively as a snig ?
I ken her fairy fabric now,
 I mark her dashing style,—
Behold ! with Nelson on her prow,
 The gallant little "Nile."

How fearlessly the tide she braves,
 How well she does her work,
She bounds above the swelling waves
 As buoyant as a cork ;

Though four feet shallows hem her round,
　Her crew serenely smile,
For she can float when others ground,—
　The saucy little " Nile."

The smoky towns their crowds disgorge;
　I hear the train's loud hum,
From heated mill and deafening forge
　Their pallid millions come;
And sickly frames with health are stored,
　And spleen forgets her bile,
And joy entrances toil, on board
　The merry little " Nile."

Here's three times three, and " one cheer more,"
　And still may fair winds waft
This water witch from shore to shore,
　Well crowded fore and aft.
Long may her owner watch her skim
　The sea, in dashing style,
And feel that she has been to him
　The grateful little " Nile."

STANZAS

To an old man on the death of his only child.

Thy heart was sad, thy looks were wan,
　Thy faith and patience sorely proved,
When death cut short Rebecca's span;
I could have wept with thee, old man,
　The loss of thy beloved.

Oh! 'twas a bitter drop to part
　From one with thee so closely blended;
No wonder if the fatal dart
Had likewise reached thy aching heart,
　And all its throbbing ended.

In fancy I could hear thee say,
    As death performed the deed of slaughter,—
" She is too young to be thy prey ;
Take me, for I am old and grey ;
    But spare, O spare my daughter ! "

Yet was thy lost Rebecca fain
    To shuffle off the mortal fetter ;
Life was to her a load of pain,
But now she feels to " die is gain,"
" To be with Christ far better."

Before she plunged in Jordan's tide
    A glimpse of Paradise was given ;
As waking from her dream she cried—
" I've seen my Joshua"—and died,
    And joined her babe in heaven.

Then hush that sob, and dry those tears ;
    She's left a Sodom, false and hollow,
Its guilt and anguish, grief and fears,
And gone, where, in a few brief years,
    Old pilgrim, thou must follow.

The future claims thy care ; arise !
    With faith unwavering, clear, and steady,
Take up thy cross, obtain the prize—
A home beyond the starry skies,
    For all things now are ready.

Earth is no long abiding place,
    For one, whose hairs are hoary :
Up, then, for at bright Canaan's gate,
Rebecca and her children wait,
    And beckon thee to glory.

STANZAS ON THE DEATH OF A YOUNG

CHRISTIAN.

How just the plea of sorrow,
　When friends resign their breath,
If man had no to-morrow
　Beyond the night of death.

Mother! on thee, while weeping,
　The word like manna falls—
" He is not dead, but sleeping,"
　To wake when Jesus calls.

Father! why art thou wearing
　A visage so depress'd,
When angel arms are bearing
　Thy darling to his rest?

The beams of glory gather
　Around his placid brow,
And with his heavenly Father,
　Dear John is happy now.

The casket there lies darkling,
　The precious gem is flown,
And faith can see it sparkling
　In the ·Redeemer's crown.

TO LITTLE HANNAH.

Thou art a pet, 'tis very clear,
To both thy parents very dear;
In their fond eyes, a sparkling pearl—
Thou little tinety, tinety, girl.

And thy Aunt Mary doth delight
To hear thee sing at morn and night,
And says—'tis wonderful how soon
" Thy cherry lips could learn a tune."

Thou hast a better friend than these—
I'll tell his name—if that will please—
His name is Jesus, and says he—
" Let little children come to me."

Once for thy sake this good friend died—
For Hannah he was crucified,
And he expects thee up above,
To dwell with him in light and love.

And " oh ! that will be joyful," grand,
To sit with him at God's right hand ;
To meet thy friends on Canaan's shore,
And ne'er lose sight of Jesus more.

TO THE SAME.

Dear Hannah—you learn from your aunt to conceal
The things that your parents do bid you reveal—
'Tis true, I am Henry, and Anderton, too,
But that's not an answer expected from you—
You, yesterday, called me a very dear name,
Which set my poor pit-a-pat heart in a flame :
Speak ! am I your " uncle ? " The truth I would know ;
I wonder who taught you to speak to me so !
I'm not so by nature ; then how can it be—
Perhaps your Aunt Mary could satisfy me !
Go ask her if she will explain how it is,
And then, Hannah —— I'll give thee a kiss.

G

TO LITTLE MARY LANGSHAW.

They say you're kind hearted—then learn to forgive
The wrong done unto thee so long as you live;
Remember that Jesus forgave thee thy debt—
Oh! learn that hard lesson—"Forgive and forget."

They say you are firm—then quite resolute be
In learning far more, love, than A B and C;
Resolve not one chance of improvement to miss,
And Father will give his good scholar a kiss.

Good-bye, Mary Langshaw, good-bye for this time,
May God, in his mercy, preserve thee from crime;
May grace unto thee, little Mary, be given,
Begun upon earth, and continued in Heaven.

FOR PETER LANGSHAW, JUN.

They tell me that eyes can distinguish and trace
Some old-fashioned folks in thy young-fashioned face;
That a look of thy Grandmother Langshaw is clear
And the features of Grandmother Philips appear.

If this be correct, then I am nothing loth
To say that thou must be a pet with them both;
But strive, my dear boy, to deserve all their love
And not their's alone, but thy Father's above.

Thy name is the name of a man great and good,
Who battled for truth and for that shed his blood;
Yet the faith of thy name-sake too hardly was tried
When with curses—thrice told—he his master denied.

May'st thou, little Peter, be valiant and bold
Like Peter, the famous disciple of old—
When he follow'd Jesus—Oh! copy it well;
But pray that thou fall not as Peter once fell.

PETER LANGSHAW.

Peter Langshaw continues uncommonly fat
And he looks very well in his Quaker-like hat ;
His wife is much thinner, but, if I may tell,
The thin one and fat one agree very well.
She's three or four sisters, and one, I avow,
Persists to my teeth that I call'd her " reet fow ;"
To silence her clapper I never will try,
But I'll stick to the fact that she tells a big lie,

TO MARY.

I've one request, sincere, yet droll,
To make to thee, my pretty Poll—
In after-times, if it should be
That thou should'st ever think of me,
Thy sweet harp from the willow take,
And sing this song for Henry's sake. :—

Long, but in vain, I've sought for rest,
    But I am restless still ;
There is a void within my heart,
    Which one alone can fill :
Dear girl ! if free to choose thou art,
    As for thy love I pine,
Take, claim, and keep my wayward heart,
    But give, Oh ! give me thine.

Through the world's garden, like a bee,
    I've hunted far and wide,
A being that would cling to me,
    When all were cold beside :
Thy heart, my Mary, is the bower
    To which I could repair,
Content to linger from this hour,
    In blessed bondage there.

My love is fixed as it appears,
　　As durable as deep;
Believe me, girl, and let these tears
　　Lull thy dark doubts to sleep.
He, who from nothing form'd this ball,
　　Knows that I do not lie;
Thou art my earthly " all in all,"
　　And shall be till I die.

How the proud world would envy me,
　　The bliss it would afford
To hear thee whisper—" let it be
　　According to thy word."
Now, Mary, now the grace impart,
　　Around my stem entwine;
" I give thee all I can "—my heart;
　　Then, give, Oh! give me thine.

TO THE SAME.

My Mary, " yet a little while," and I must go from thee,
And deep will be the parting sigh that hour will draw
　　from me;
Not often in this heartless world, is it my hap to wile
My carking cares away with one, who can so sweetly smile.

Yes! when that bitter hour shall come, I shall not so regret
Thy beauty, as thy kind heart, which dares me to forget;
Would that thy heart was mine, for then, wherever I might
　　rove,
Our joined souls might rest in all the confidence of love.

'Tis sweet to have a friend indeed, in whom we may confide,
One, in whose blest companionship, away my life might
　　glide;
But sweeter far to win a soul, with pure affection rife,
In gladness and in sorrow, too, the angel of my life.

And go I must, yet ere I go, oh ! let me call my own,
*   *   *   (and so sweet to hear) thy voice's silver tone ;
Oh ! let thy short and fond response, with exultation swell,
My trembling, scarcely hoping heart, before I breathe—
"Farewell."

TO MARY

On hearing her say " I wish I was in Heaven."

"I wish I was in Heaven"—well go !
   And leave my stricken soul to vent
To friendless ears her tale of woe
   And lonely discontent.

Go ! pass the bounds that separate
   This troublous speck from that blest shore,
Where mortal love shall agitate
   Thy vigin soul no more !

Go! if the pictured scenes we drew
   Of what our wedded life should be ;
If all's forgot, thy track pursue ;
   Nor heed my misery.

Go ! reckless of my tears and sighs ;
   Go ! though thy absence is my hell ;
Go ! if thou'rt ready, to yon skies,
   And I will gasp "farewell !"

I ne'er was happy at the best ;
   And what brief gleams of joy were mine
Were garner'd in a faithful breast;
   And whose that breast but thine ?

Like a nail fast in a sure place
   Am I to thee ; and didst thou not
Vow, with me to run life's brief race,
   And soothe my thorny lot ?

Oh, by that well remembered vow,
  By thy given heart—a blessed boon—
Why was it given ? And why wilt thou
  Take back thy gift so soon ?

I bargained with thee, love for love,
  And paid mine down, warm, gushing, fond ;
Discharge the debt which thus I prove,
  For "I will have my bond."

"I wish I was in heaven," thou sayst ;
  Why that's my earnest prayer; and when
This heart account is paid thou mayst,
  But stir not hence till then.

"Pay what thou owest," and when all's right,
  And mine acquittance sets thee free,
Then, Mary, wing thy upward flight,
  And I will fly with thee.

TO MARY.

When Mary's spirit, panting for the skies,
  Left tenantless her fair abode of clay ;
I dare not watch the grave side obsequies,
  I dare not look where her discarded relics lay.
And now, when two long years have fleeted by
  A keen remembrance will sometimes awaken
My startled soul, and force a heaving sigh,
  And shake a heart, by aught besides unshaken.

"Time tempers sorrow ;" it may lull awhile,
  But not eradicate the sense of grief ;
And even I, who smile when others smile,
  Have sorrows which admit of no relief ;
For so ill-starr'd has been my destiny,
  My brightest prospects in the bud were blighted,
And cheerfulness and pleasure fly from me
  As one to dark despondency united.

TO FANNY.

"Actions speak louder far than words."
How sweet a hope this truth affords !
To doubt thee now would be unjust,
Thy whisper'd tenderness I'll trust,
Thy "actions" shall my surety be,
That, as I love, thou lovest me.

Thy father kind, with anguish torn,
Will grieve to lose his youngest born ;
An honest sigh will Rachel heave
When thou shalt take thy life-long leave ;
And sad the moment when ye part
Will press on Lydia's gentle heart.

And I shall make this sacrifice
For "home, sweet home," I fondly prize ;
And grief will wring my heart to hear
The last farewell of friends so dear ;
Yet I can freely all resign
To have thee here, and call thee mine.

Yes, Fanny, we must all forsake,
But sweeter, stronger, ties we'll make ;
And here, upon the ocean's breast,
We build our temporary nest,
And to the heartless worldling prove
How blest are they who truly love.

Yet, think not, dearest, to attain
A lot on earth exempt from pain ;
Sin hath so marr'd our prospects fair,
That pain and pleasure, joy and care,
Are mingled for us—since the fall ;
But love will make amends for all.

And if the God of Grace, the while,
Should bless our union with his smile;
Nor choicer favour shall we need,
Till from this narrow prison freed,
When to our native home we soar
To live and love for evermore.

TO MRS. ANDERTON.

Thy lot with mine is cast,
   Our hearts are plighted,
And if we be as fast
   To Christ united,
We shall enjoy below
What worldlings never know,
A heaven before we go
   To dwell in glory.

And though on earth we meet
   With stormy weather,
Where bitter things and sweet
   Are mix'd together;
My voice shall lull thy fears,
My hand shall dry thy tears,
While Faith our vessel steers
   Straight home to glory.

Misfortunes may come on,
   And sickness seize us,
But if we two are one,
   And "one in Jesus;"
His word this truth maintains,
That after all our pains
A sweeter rest remains
   For us in glory.

Weep not! though death at length
 Our ties will shiver,
For Faith will lend us strength
 To cross the river,
And we shall recognise
Each other in the skies,
When Christ shall say, ''Arise!
 And share my glory!''

TO MISS A. D.

Strange thoughts, dear Anne, would fill your head
When told that Fanny Snape was wed,
You'd be in tune to laugh or cry,
You'd think your friend was very shy,
And feel dispos'd to take this text—
'' I wonder what will happen next.''

Yet, though she bears another name,
Poor Fanny's heart is still the same
As when ye went, with converse sweet,
Linked arm in arm, up Cannon-street,—
Or leaving tracts ye pass'd away
The ever-welcome Sabbath Day.

'' And is she happy?'' you will ask,
Yes, Anne,—beneath God's smile we bask,
And urg'd by love, we gladly share,
Each other's joy, each other's care;
Our life runs smoothly, like a rill,
And we are busy courting still.

Go, search the whole creation round,
Two more united can't be found,
Me, to the world, our Fan prefers,
My life is fast bound up in hers;
As cheerful as the birds are we,
And, if you doubt it, '' Come and see.''

"Come Anne," says Fanny, "and admire
Our home at Fleetwood-on-the-Wyre;"
"Come Anne," say I, "and gaze upon
A home where truly two are one:"
Thus may God's blessing ever dwell
With you and your's, and fare-ye-well!

TO MARGARET.

Where is thy sister? not on earth,
    In this low "vale of tears,"
That voice of sweet and guileless mirth
    No more shall bless thy ears;
And thou mayst weep as one bereft,
    Then let thy grief-drops flow,
And thou mayst smile, for she has left
    Her heritage of woe.

She has "shuffled off this mortal coil,"
    And her deserted clay
Is made the "last destroyer's" spoil
    In mouldering decay,—
Her earthly tortures were extreme,
    And her mortal eye wax'd dim,—
But Jesus suffer'd to redeem,
    And her "mind's eye" gaz'd on him.

Then treasure up her dying words,
    Let them thy heart revive,
That retrospect a hope affords,
    That Jane "is yet alive."
Before thy beauteous sister died,
    Ere yet her soul was freed,
"He ever lives above," she cried,
    "For me to intercede."

Margaret, where is thy sister now ?
  With the shining ranks of grace,
The " crown of life " relumes her brow,
  And glory decks her face ;
Oh ! may that soaring soul be fraught
  With energy divine,
To make her Saviour, and her lot,
  For ever, ever thine.

Margaret ! I have perused her life,
  Whose matchless zeal these pages prove ;
An angel in a world of strife,
  A martyr in the cause of love.
She was a chosen one of God,
  She felt the Saviour always near,
She proved the power of Jesu's blood,
  She found " the love that casts out fear !"

Where is she now ? Where Jesus is,
  Where sin and sorrow may not come ;
In heaven—that heritage of bliss ;
  In Zion—her " abiding home."
Oh, in our life's day
  We have a glorious work to do ;
Then let us track her shining way,
  That we may dwell with Jesus, too.

LINES

Addressed to the Widow and Daughter of the late

Richard Stephenson.

Why do those heavy floods of sorrow gather
  In eyes, where late bright smiles were seen to play ?
They flow for him,—the husband, friend and father,
  By death's rude summons rudely snatch'd away.

A husband,—faithful to his first embraces,
  A father,—sway'd by gentleness benign,
A man,—whose earthly love and moral graces
  Were fashion'd in the moulds of love divine.

Oh, bitter stroke, all power of words excelling!
  To lose a husband, father, friend, like this,
For never soul resign'd the fleshly dwelling
  More loving, or more fondly lov'd, than his.

Yea, while you raise the voice of lamentation,
  I, too, will grieve because that tongue is mute,
Which, tun'd by Jesus and his "great salvation,"
  Hath match'd Isaiah's lyre or David's lute.

But what, though Death all human ties can sever,
  The soul defies the tyrant's stern embrace,
Believers only die to live for ever
  With Jesus, their Redeemer, "face to face."

The way to life lies through the grave's dim portal,—
  And oh, what joy doth this sweet truth afford;
Our buried friend survives—a free immortal,
  Cloth'd in a "glorious body" like the Lord.

Poor, lonely widow! toss'd by every billow,
  Why grieve for one so honour'd, safe, and blest?
The Lamb,—now thy husband—go and pillow
  Thy throbbing heart upon his bleeding breast.

Thou weepest, Anne! and reason cannot blame thee,
  Yet, doff that sackcloth for a garb less wild,—
The orphan's Father will adopt and claim thee
  When thou art willing to become His child.

Oh! would you share the home that he inherits,
  Whose spirit hath just dropp'd the cumbrous clod,
Make good your claim, through the Redeemer's merits,
  And, strong in faith, "Prepare to meet your God."

TO —— AND HIS SISTERS ON THE

SUDDEN DEATH OF THEIR PARENTS.

Poor orphans—twice bereft!
With all your living " troop" of friends, no other
Can fill the gap left by the cherished dead—
Your kind dear father with the silver'd head,
And your sweet mother.

The grave's serene eclipse,
As with a sable curtain, shadeth
From your tear-laden and corporeal glance
Those dear ones—in bright inheritance,
Which never fadeth.

How sorrowful to you,
How beautiful to them, was this transition,
When, as they passed the dim and shadowy maze,
The Golden City's clear and glittering blaze
Fill'd their rapt vision.

Children, your grief repress,
Nor yield that deep, expressive scope to sorrow :
Like them, for your mysterious change prepare,
That, after death's brief midnight, ye may share
Their bright to-morrow.

Would ye the last recal,
To this dread Golgotha and weeping,
From a retreat so tearless, calm and pure,
Where Jesus hath the " little flock" secure
In His own keeping ?

Excessive grief is vain.
Ye know earth's seeming evergreens must wither
Beyond time's limits, and the dark'ning form
Of Jordan is your parent's happy home—
Go track them thither !

ON THE DEATH OF A YOUNG FRIEND.

Addressed to her Parents.

Why should you mourn, with unavailing sorrow,
   The loss of one, whom skill nor prayers could save?
Why load your souls with hopelessness, and borrow
   The black and dismal aspect of the grave?

If, by this life, man's destiny was bounded;
   If, like the brutes, your dear departed slept;
Reason might own your sad complaints well grounded,
   Nor blame the sigh you heav'd, the tear you wept.

If, by death's irrespective slaughter,
   Our dreams of "something" after death were cross'd,
Then might her parents mourn their vanish'd daughter—
   Their sleeping child as one for ever lost.

But, if at death, the unharm'd spirit smileth,
   Your mourning hush, your bitter tear-drops spare;
For there, "where nothing enters that defileth,"
   Your young immortal breathes her native air.

Even while I muse with that glad, chasten'd feeling,
   Which hopes like this to trusting souls impart,
Methinks I hear sweet consolation stealing
   Like heaven's own music to my ravish'd heart.

'Tis her dear voice—for it can be no other—
   "Let not your hearts," she cries, "so troubled be
Rejoice, my dear father, and be glad my mother,
   For all is well; arise, and follow me."

RUTH JOHNSON BLAND, ÆT. 21.

Death is sin's penalty ;
  Nor youth, nor hoary hairs,
Can claim exemption from his shafts
  Who pities not, nor spares ;
He smites the sweet and guiltless babe,
  The sinner old in crime ;
The maiden in her morning bloom,
  And manhood in his prime.

The cloud that hung o'er Chesham Mount
  Has deepen'd into gloom,
Since beauty, youth, and gentle worth
  Have glided to the tomb ;
Nor father's groans, nor mother's tears,
  Nor lover's bitter sighs,
Could longer keep the captive here—
  This angel from the skies.

The painful strife is ended now,
  The weary voyage o'er,
And long ere this her love-borne steps
  Have touched a brighter shore ;
Past the dim out-let of the grave
  Souls breathe their native air ;
And faith assures her wailing friends
  That Ruth is shining there.

Ah ! cruel was this wrench of hearts,
  Yet mercy dealt the blow,
For lingering years were lingering pain—
  A heritage of woe ;
But shiver'd is the golden bowl,
  The worn-out frame is still,
And pillow'd in serene repose,
  She sleeps on Bircle Hill ;

A sure retreat—a glad escape—
  From sorrow, death, and pain;
From racking cough, and languid pulse,
  And throbbing heart aud brain:
The Saviour woo'd the stricken lamb
  To his own fold above;
Oh! what a shelter are the arms
  Of Everlasting Love.

Her happy soul has thrown aside
  The garments of decay;
This fragrant flower, which wither'd here,
  Blooms in Eternal day;
A chrysalis has burst her shell,
  And upward—God-ward flown—
Another glittering gem is set
  In the Redeemer's Crown.

Her early doom should startle us
  Who sadly linger here;
Health hopes a longer lease of life,
  Yet death is lurking near;
The frequent hearse, the daily bell,
  The hourly lifted sod,
In solemn, thrilling, accents cry
  "Prepare to meet your God."

TO MR. ROBERT SNAPE,

On hearing that he had entered upon his 69th year.

"Being confident of this very thing—that he who hath begun a
good work in us, will perform it, unto the day of the Lord Jesus
Christ."—ST. PAUL.

"Three-score and ten!" such is the span
That measures out the life of man;
Not long, then, must thou here abide,
For God—thy Father, Friend, and Guide—
Hath led thee eight-and-sixty years
Through this low vale of sin and tears.

" The time of thy departure's near,"
Nor dost thou wish to linger here;
Thy weary spirit does not shrink
From Jordan's fast approaching brink,
For Jesus—good and " strong to save"—
Can bear thee safely o'er the wave.

Eternal life—the long sought prize,
Beyond that gloomy river lies,
And wildly though its billows roll,
They will not overwhelm thy soul,
For, after all thy trials past,
God will not fail thee at the last.

Thus saith the Lord, and says to thee
" Where I am you shall also be ;"
As sure as He thy peace hath made,
As sure as He thy debt hath paid,
His work in thee He can defend,
And will perform it to the end.

Thy trembling steps—thy hair so grey—
Proclaim thy mortal frame's decay,
Thy sin-sick soul, by cares oppress'd,
Like thy poor body, pines for rest,
And Simeon's words are in thy heart—
" Lord let thy servant now depart."

Thy time is near, yet there's one thing
That chains thee here, and clips thy wing,
And thus thy thoughts break out afresh,
" Lord! save my children in the flesh,
Let all, like me, thy mercy find ;"
And let not one be left behind.

God is a God that answers prayer—
Then leave thy children to His care ;
The grace that pull'd the father thro'—
Can reach and bless his children too,
Graft them to Israel's chosen stock,
And add them to His " little flock."

H

Then give thy doubtings to the wind,
Leave earth, and earth-born cares, behind,
Thy Saviour calls by day and night,
Press to that "land of pure delight,"
And when at "home, sweet home," prepare
To welcome all thy children there.

LOVE SONG.

I'll lock thee, dearest, in my heart,
And thou shalt be my better part ;
I'll cling to thee ; and as the dove
May die, but cannot change his love,
So shall my soul devoted be
To thee, dear girl, and none but thee.

I cannot, as the changeful do,
Make a long love speech, when I woo ;
I cannot, like a trifler, show
More than I feel ; but this I know,
Though greater beauties I may see,
My heart desireth none but thee.

More ruby lips might pout to bless
Mine, with their ripe voluptuousness ;
And eyes more flashing may conspire
To turn away my fixed desire ;
Yet from such elves secure and free,
I'll bend, dear girl, to none but thee.

Time may roll on, as it hath rolled,
And change the scenes we now behold ;
Yet as the needle to the pole
Points evermore, so shall my soul
Direct her gaze, through life's rough sea,
And find a home in none but thee.

Then cheer thee, though awhile we part,
Strange eyes shall not estrange my heart;
Though farewell tears thy cheeks bedew,
Believe me, love, as thou art true;
And think, that severed though we be,
My spirit yearns for none but thee.

THIRST, AND ITS TRUE ANTIDOTE.

As water ranks, by all the world confess'd,
Of nature's boons, the greatest and the best,
So, in her catalogue of ills, the first
Is fierce, unmixed, unmitigable thirst;
Lo! when the fleshy pores too widely gape,
Through which the streams of vital juice escape,
The vital heat, which nothing then restrains,
Rolls the hot blood like lava through the veins;
And thick eruptions on the parched skin
Are symptomatic of the pangs within;
A raging Etna of intense desire,
Whose flames are hotter than material fire.
Oh, dread sensation! restless, maddening, wild,
Compared with which stern hunger's tooth is mild.
Oh, wretched state, of human woes the chief,
When man would swallow poison for relief;
And one cool draught from nature's sparkling rills
Is worth "the cattle on a thousand hills."

SONG.

Yes, distance makes the love we bear
  Our cherished friends increase;
It often calls the heart-sent tear
  To flow and rarely cease.

And thus, dear girl, does my sad soul
    Bow to respond to thine ;
Oh, do thy gentle musings roll
    In unison with mine ?

My heart of hearts, in its least strain'd,
    And least impure recess ;
There, friend, hast thou for ever reign'd
    In growing loveliness !

And oft amid the cares of life,
    Which often ruffle me,
With which our pilgrimage is rife,
    I'll breathe a prayer for thee.

Oh, does thy mental vision swim
    With hours so sweet, but gone ?
And dost thou ever think of him
    Who's grieving all alone ?

He was thy friend, he still is so ;
    This simple song will tell
How pure and changeless is the glow
    That warms his heart—" Farewell."

A BLESSING.

By our merciful Creator
    We, poor helpless worms, are led
To the banquet-house of nature
    Kindly to be cloth'd and fed ;
        Heavenly Father
    Give us still our daily bread.

For the bounties amply given,
    Help us some return to make ;
Grant that of the bread of heaven
    Freely we may now partake ;
        Make us welcome
    To that feast, for Jesus' sake.

A BLESSING.

Still kept by thy kind power, we live,
Unworthy though we be ;
And still, dear Father, we receive
Our daily bread from thee.

Oh, sanctify, indulgent Lord,
The bounties thou hast given;
And grant that all who crowd this board
May taste thy love in Heaven !

HYMNS

Sung on the occasion of laying the Foundation Stone of the

Temperance Hall, Bolton, May 24th, 1839.

HYMN FIRST.

BEFORE LAYING THE STONE.

Vice lords it o'er this Christian land,
Her man-traps set and baited stand,
 To catch unwary souls ;
And " seeking whom he may devour,"
With serpent guile, and boundless power,
 The " roaring lion" prowls.

Till late, the servants of the Lord,
Forbore to wield the two-edged sword—
 In blameful slumber laid,—
Though every drunkard, dead and lost,
Was purchased at so great a cost,
 On Calvary's summit paid.

Awaking from that guilty trance,
Behold! our Temperance ranks advance!
    Our cross-mark'd banners wave;
And on this spot we pitch our tent,
The schemes of hell to circumvent,
    And liberate the slave!

Yet, firmly though the stone we plant,
Unless the Lord the increase grant,
    How barren our employ!
Lord! make the truths proclaimed here,
To hapless drunkards far and near,
    "Glad tidings of great joy."

A life-boat may our temple be,
For thousands toss'd upon the sea
    Of lust, and shame, and sin;
For them and theirs a refuge prove,
A stepping-stone to Jesu's love,—
    For all who enter in.

From drunkards who have mercy found,
Oft may our Temperance Hall resound,
    With shouts of holy mirth;
And Bolton, now so sunk in crime,
Become, like Zion of old time,
    A praise in all the earth.

HYMN SECOND.

AFTER LAYING THE STONE.

The Stone is laid, whereon, we trust,
    A refuge shall be built;
To which the frenzied sons of lust,
    Will fly from chains and guilt.

Here contrite reprobates shall mourn
　Who never wept before;
And, trembling for their souls, return,
　Resolve to "sin no more."

Here shall their wives and children meet,
　To speak of joys restored;
And join their neighbours in a sweet
　Hosanna to the Lord.

Here shall backsliders, sick in soul,
　Bewail their guilt and loss;
And, yearning for salvation, roll
　Their burdens on the cross.

Thy glory, and the weal of man,
　To these our hopes aspire;
Our efforts, Lord! with favour scan,
　And grant our hearts' desire.

Are not the souls of drunkards Thine?
　Thine for a price paid down?
Lord! fit them evermore to shine
　Bright jewels in Thy crown.

HYMN FOR GOOD FRIDAY.

Thou Son of David and his Lord,
　Where shall a sinner rest?
Where hide his load of guilt abhorr'd,
　But in thy willing breast?

For me, in crimson drops, that sweat
　By Kedron's brook ran down;
And on thy head in mockery sat
　The sharp and thorny crown.

Thy limbs were rent by Pilate's lash
   For me—a child of hell ;
And on thy head the lightning flash
   Of God's displeasure fell.

Thy merits magnified the law,
   That God might man forgive ;
Thy richest blood did freely flow
   That these " dry bones" might live.

Thy death left hope where none was found ;
   Made peace where there was strife ;
And on thy dying pangs I ground
   My claim to endless life.

No other refuge, Lord, have I,
   But in thy gushing side ;
My Jesus, lifted up on high,
   Emmanuel crucified !

Extend to me thy mercy now,
   By thy dear cross and pain ;
Thy smitten face and bleeding brow
   Let me not see in vain.

Grant me the boon bestowed on him,
   Who stretched upon the tree,
As life's last glimmer grew more dim,
   Cried, " Lord, remember me !"

Remember me, thou Source of Grace,
   And, guided by thy love,
My soul shall reach her native place,
   Our " home, sweet home," above.

A HYMN.

"REJOICE IN THE LORD, ALWAY."

What hath the saint to do with gloom ?
  The willing slave of sin
May tremble at his coming doom,
  The danger he is in.

'Tis just that our Redeemer's foes
  Should feel his flaming sword ;
But safety is the lot of those
  Whose " trust is in the Lord."

Does not our God, in accents mild,
  This declaration make—
" The soul whom grace hath reconciled
  I never will forsake ? "

Joint heir with Jesus of that place,
  Which never can decay ;
Rejoice ! for thine's a happy case,
  And dash thy tears away.

A HYMN.

Tune—" Alarm.'

Why lag, ye sinners, on the road,
So burden'd with that heavy load ?
Awake ! awake ! delay's a crime,
Make for the Refuge, while there's time !

This way conducts to joy and peace,
And that to woes that never cease ;
Resolve ! resolve ! begin the strife
For hell or glory, death or life !

Yet never on that journey start
With guilty mind or lep'rous heart ;
The cross ! the cross ! to that repair
And hang your burdens boldly there !

Straight is the way, and long beside,
But Jesus is a matchless guide ;
" My blood ! my blood !"—our leader cries,
" Is a sure passport to the skies !"

Then free from sin's detested yoke,
Your mind at peace, your shackles broke,
March on ! march on ! to that bright shore,
Where sheep and shepherd part no more !

EVENING HYMN.

Tune—" Good night."

To weary man repose is sweet,
  A blessing we'll not slight,
But give to God the praises meet,
  Before we say " Good night."

We thank thee, in this peaceful hour,
  Thou Source of Grace and Might,
By whose " one offering" we have power
  To bid " the curse" " Good night."

Should'st thou thy favour, Lord, remove,
  How helpless then our plight ;
But, trusting in thy covenant love,
  We bid our fears " Good night."

Oh, Lord, our cold dark hearts inflame
  And fill with heavenly light,
That we in thy most holy name,
  May bid our sins " Good night."

If we are thine, approaching death
  Will not our souls affright,
But joyfully our dying breath
  Shall bid the world " Good night."

And when at length, the struggle o'er,
  Our spirits take their flight,
We'll meet in heaven to part no more,
  And never say " Good night."

THE RIVER OF DEATH.

Lo ! a dread, a burning river,
  Overwhelms the land by stealth !
And its headlong currents shiver
  All the props of cherish'd wealth !
    All affection,
  Reason, piety, and health !

In this frightful, flowing terror,
  This dread feeder of the tomb !
Myriads, ere they see their error,
  Perish in its death-fraught womb !
    Thus, unpardon'd,
  Rushing to their endless doom.

Where is this destructive water, '
  Ruinous to a world so fair ?
Where these victims of self-slaughter
  Wooing hell's unmix'd despair ?
    Find a drunkard,
  And behold a victim there.

Yes ! intemp'rance is that torrent,
  Mortals quaff its direful wave,
Rush to crimes the most abhorrent !
  Plunge into a hopeless grave !
    Madly heedless
  Of the Saviour's power to save.

Could I tamely see another,
    Sink the roaring waves beneath?
Can a Christian see a brother
    Prematurely stop his breath,
        Without striving
    To prevent the " second death?"

Men! this vice has spoil'd man's beauty,
    From this blight your country purge;
It is every Christian's duty;
    Sure 'tis needless more to urge;
        Free your country
    From this desolating scourge!

God, beneath thy broad protection,
    Let the cause of temp'rance be;
Fill the drunkard with reflection,
    Set his spell-bound spirit free
        Save him, Jesus!
    Fit him for eternity.

THE TRIUMPHS OF SOBRIETY.

Lift up your hearts, and voices too,
To Him to whom the praise is due;
And let the glorious subject be—
The triumphs of sobriety.

What has it done? Delightful things,
Beyond our best imaginings;
The Ethiop's white, the lion's tam'd—
And hoary drunkards are reclaim'd.

This is the great deliverance,
Achiev'd by God, through temperance;
And can the Christian ever cease
To pray, to work for its increase?

Christians! this very hour begin
To check our land's peculiar sin;
And seek his aid who can afford—
The aid of an Almighty Lord.

———

AN APPEAL TO THE TRUE FRIENDS OF ZION.

PART FIRST.

Lo! Zion droops—in vain—in vain,
  Her temple gates are opened wide;
Intemp'rance blights her fair domain,
  And lures ten thousand from her side.

In vain her watchmen cry aloud,
  And urge their plea with many tears;
They cannot pierce the drunken crowd,
  Who shun God's house and close their ears.

They cannot see—intemp'rance blinds
  The hoary sire and beardless youth;
Then how can their bewilder'd minds
  Preceive or feel the force of truth!

To Salem's court they never wend,
  Far from her sacred fane they rove;
At Jesu's shrine they never bend;
  Nor list "his still small voice of love."

And well may Zion hang her head,
  Griev'd for her trump's neglected sound,
When such an upas tree can spread
  Its mortal taint on all around.

PART SECOND.

Yet fallen as the drunkard is,
    Though fallen he is our brother still ;
For him our Lord left heaven's bliss,
    And bled on Calvary's rugged hill.

Hark ! heard ye not that woe-fraught cry ?
    From Jesu's lips that wail proceeds ;
Eli—Lama—Sabacthani—
    The sinless for the sinful bleeds.

If He, who was all free from sin,
    From yon bright realms of bliss withdrew,
To welcome even drunkards in,
    Shall we not love the drunkard too ?

And if the truths of scripture are
    Impervious to his clouded mind ;
'Tis ours to wage incessant war
    With the foul sin that makes him blind.

For never till this foe be driven,
    Shall Sharon's rose the world perfume ;
Nor hope, the beacon light of heaven,
    The drunkard's darken'd soul illume.

Lovers of Zion ! foes of hell,
    Ye who for Christ count all things lost,
Strengthen our hands ; we seek to swell
    The bloodless triumphs of the cross.

Rouse from your slumber, catch our zeal,
    Our weapon is the written word ;
Our only guerdon Zion's weal ;
    Our aim, the glory of the Lord !

WHAT IS A DRUNKARD.

What is a drunkard ? One who quaffs
Reason-expelling drugs ; and laughs
    At every holy thing ;
The "Prince of Air's" unquestioned prize ;
At whose approach religion flies,
    With an affrighted wing.

What is a drunkard ? Passion's dupe,
Whose worse than brutal cravings stoop
    "To drain the maddening bowl;"
Who gratifies his swine-like lust ;
And when he does it knows he must
    Ensnare his deathless soul.

What is a drunkard ? Read his life
In the dejection of his wife,
    His children pale and wan ;
And looking, thief-like at his feet,
With dire remorselessness replete,
    Behold, behold the man !

What is a drunkard ? One who dares
God's fierce displeasure, and whose prayers
    Are " curses loud and deep ;"
Whose callousness increases still,
Albeit he knows his madness will
    Undying tortures reap.

What is a drunkard ? One for whom
The Lord descended to the tomb,
    For whom our ransom died ;
And shall we not who bear the name
Of Jesus, labour to reclaim
    The gradual suicide !

O God, the merciful as just!
While for our sins we lick the dust ;
   Yet for thy first-born's sake,
O bless the cause of temperance here,
Stay drunkards in their mad career,
   And let thine arm awake !

THE DRUNKARD'S WIFE.

Tune—" The Soldier's Tear."

Before the altar stood
   The bridegroom and the bride,
With willing hands and blended hearts,
   The holy knot was tied;
   And when he spake the words,
   So welcome and so dear,
There glistened in her mild blue eye
   That test of love—a tear.

   And thus they liv'd and loved—
   The hours were never dull,
And heaven crowned their happy love,
   With pledges beautiful ;
   And as her charge increased,
   With each succeeding year,
The mother's heart rushed to her eye,
   Which trembled with a tear.

   But year has followed year—
   As wave succeeding wave—
The once-loved wife is joyless now,
   And he a drunken slave ;
   Vice o'er him holds her sway,
   And from his dark career
She tries to win him, and her eye—
   Her dimm'd eye drops a tear.

Her kindness pleads in vain—
His heart is seared and hard,
And tauntings loud, and cruel blows,
Are that fond wife's reward ;
He spurns her from his side,
With look and word severe,
Yet, for that ruffian's sake, her eye
Is gushing with a tear.

Upon his dying couch,
Fear wraps his soul in gloom,
When common friendship hides her head,
She never leaves the room ;
She kneels, and if faith can
Compel the Lord to hear,
She opens mercy's gate and melts
The sinner with a tear.

That wife's a widow now ;
The star of hope shall rise
No more for her ; her bosom lord
Died as the drunkard dies !
God help this bruised reed,
Her load of woe to bear !
For none but thou can rest her soul,
Who cannot shed a tear.

THE DYING DRUNKARD.

Stretch'd on a heap of straw—his bed,
The dying drunkard lies ;
His joyless wife supports his head,
And to console him tries :
His weeping children's love would ease
His spirit, but in vain ;
Their ill-paid love destroys his peace ;
He'll never smile again.

I

His boon companions—where arc they,
 Who shar'd his heart and bowl?
Yet come not nigh to charm away
 The horrors from his soul.
What have such friends to do with those
 Who press the couch of pain?
And he is rack'd with mortal throes—
 He'll never rise again.

And where is mercy in that hour
 Of dread, and pain, and guilt?
Though Jesu's blood, of matchless power,
 For man's sear'd soul was spilt—
If justice spurn the fear-urg'd prayer,
 For him't has flow'd in vain;
And lock'd in thy embrace, despair,
 He'll never hope again.

TO THE DRUNKARD.

Besotted slave, by lust o'erpower'd,
 Repent, or dark thy doom will be;
The dullest cloud that ever lower'd
   Now bursts on thee.
Souls die not with departing breath,
 And wilt thou trust that sceptic prop?
There is a worse, a second death—
   Stop! madman, stop!

There is another after life,
 Where hope is swallowed in despair,
And bootless is the sinner's strife,
   For mercy there.
Time flies—life wanes—and demons wait
 To bear thee off,—a helpless prize;
Oh! ere the effort be too late,
   Rise! drunkard, rise!

APPEAL TO CHRISTIANS.

Why stand ye idle all the day—
  While drunkards, an unnumber'd host,
Madly with their perdition play—
  Die without pardon, and are lost ?

The true saint never thinks of self,
  When battling with a damning vice;
But gladly parts with time and pelf,
  If God demand the sacrifice.

As Christ for him; so he for such
  As have by guilt heaven's anger brav'd,
Should give up all, nor deem it much—
  E'en nought—if drunkards can be saved.

Diseased without, diseased within,
  Their case a heart of flint would melt;
Have pity on these slaves of sin,
  Ye, who Messiah's power have felt.

He paid your debt's extreme demands,
  When hell's dread prison gap'd for you,
For Christ's sake seize your brother ' brands,'
  And ' snatch them from the burning ' too.

Oh ! while the sot to ruin drives,
  Point out to him a safer track;
And, by the magnet of your lives,
  Attract these lust-born truants back.

Poor Zion mourns her scattered sheep;
  And can her shepherds sleep supine ?
The fields are white, and who should reap ?
  Servant of God! the work is thine.

CHRISTIAN EXPEDIENCE.

PART FIRST.

When death unties the gordian knot
  There is beyond life's dwindling span
An after state—a dateless lot—
  A long eternity for man.

Yet, mortals plunge in blackest crime,
  Abuse the span in mercy given;
And sell " eternity for time,"
  As if there were no hell—nor heaven.

For pleasures that repentance bring,
  For joys that tarry not a day,
Our drunken fellow-sinners fling
  Life, everlasting life, away.

And Zion wails her heavy loss,
  And Lebanon her cedars fell'd;
For by deserters from the cross,
  Damnation's reeling ranks are swell'd.

Can we this mortal havoc view,
  And feel no pain and shed no tears ?
Nor weeping, ask " What shall they do,
  When Christ, the righteous judge, appears ?"

Does not, as on " these slain " we look,
  The still small voice of conscience cry :
" Our own examples bait the hook,
  Which weaker brethren sieze and die ?"

PART SECOND.

We cannot pray dead drunkards back,
    But lives in self denial spent
May lure the living from the track
    That thousands, now in torment, went.

" I'll not eat flesh," writes gen'rous Paul,
    (Who knew and did his duty well),
" Lest by my right our brothers fall,
    Or drunkards stumble into hell.

As he abstain'd—we likewise must
    Dash from our trembling lips the bowl,
And trample on that fleshly lust,
    Which wars against the drunkard's soul.

Weak is the Christian's faith who deems
    These " dead alive " too deeply gone :
Blood, blood enough to save them streams
    From the rent heart of God's dear Son.

But oh, a parting must take place,
    The drunkard from his deeds obscene,
Before the troubled pool of grace
    Can wash the filthy leper clean.

Lord, teach us so our course to shape
    That our " pure living " may inspire
Our brethren with a wish to 'scape
    The vengeance of eternal fire.

CHRISTIAN EFFORTS TO RECLAIM THE

INTEMPERATE.

Drunkards sleep—the sword hangs o'er them.
　Brethren ! your example give—
Let your light so shine before them,
　That they may repent and live ;
Habit, with her mountain barriers,
　Chokes their path—without delay
Break them down, ye gospel warriors !
　Take the stumbling block away.

Fathers, husbands, sons, and brothers,
　Laden with this heavy doom,
Sisters, daughters, wives, and mothers,
　Sink hopeless to the tomb ;
Sin's " broad way " with victims crowded,
　Homes despoil'd, and millions too,
By the winding sheet enshrouded,
　From their graves—appeal to you !

By the ties this voice hath riven,
　By the homes this sin hath marr'd,
By the souls this curse hath driven
　Unreclaim'd to their reward ;
By the earth, which it is thinning,
　By the hell which ends it track,
Use your influence with the sinning,
　Guide your Father's stray sheep back.

What, though for these lost immortals,
　Blood from Calv'ry's fount may gush,
Thousands perish—hell's wide portals
　Gape for them and down they rush.
Lo ! through error's devious turnings,
　See what fearful speed they make ;
From the " everlasting burnings,"
　Save them for your Master's sake.

THE DRUNKARD RAISED.

What numbers for the deadly glass,
  Sell soul—and body—too ;
Forgive them, Father, for alas !
  They know not what they do.

Assist us, Lord, these souls to win,
  The drunkard's soul to save,
To crush the land's besetting sin,
  And free the struggling slave.

Display thine arm, Almighty power,
  And strike a winning blow !
The captive free—and from this hour
  " Loose him, and let him go."

CHRIST DIED FOR DRUNKARDS.

Ye, who for souls immortal strive,
  Arise, and form a temperance band,
By Jesus led, equipp'd to drive
  The horrid monster from the land.

How many feel his gripe, and lo !
  The priest and Levite pass them by,
And Christians self-securely go,
  Nor cast aside a pitying eye.

Yet, left as drunkards are, alone,
  Their souls were bought with Jesu's blood ;
For them the garden heard his groan,
  And gushed for them the purple flood.

But lead by drink—accursed drink—
   What crowds their hell-ward journey take,
And madly sport on ruin's brink—
   Lead, lead them back for Jesu's sake.

Oh, teach them "not to touch nor taste,"
   Lest hell should seize what mercy claims;
Haste to their rescue,—Jesus—haste,
   . And snatch thy purchase from the flames.

APPEAL TO DRUNKARDS.

Drunkard! can thy soul forget,
Him who paid thy mighty debt
Him extended on the tree—
Stretch'd and nail'd and pierc'd for thee ?

Thou art sick—and He can cure ;
To that fountain deep and pure,
Crimson with redeeming gore,
Brother !—" Go, and sin no more."

THE END.

W. AND J. DOBSON, PRINTERS, PRESTON.